M000032151

THE FAERIE MATES

DARK WORLD: THE FAERIE GAMES 3

MICHELLE MADOW

DREAMSCAPE PUBLISHING

~CHARACTER LIST~

Selena Pearce: Chosen champion of Jupiter, the king of the gods. Lightning magic. Half faerie, half witch. Her faerie magic is bound and her witch magic has yet to show. Adopted daughter of Queen Annika and Prince Jacen Pearce. Biological daughter of Prince Devyn Kavanagh and Camelia Conrad. Soulmate of Julian Kane. Lives in Avalon, but has been kidnapped to the Otherworld.

Julian Kane: Chosen champion of Mars, the god of war. Combat magic, and the ability to pull weapons from the ether. Half-blood faerie, with bound faerie magic. Soulmate of Selena Pearce. Lives in the Otherworld.

Torrence Devereux: Witch. Daughter of Amber Devereux and an unnamed father. Best friend of Selena Pearce. Lives in Avalon during the weekdays, and at the Devereux mansion in Beverly Hills on the weekends.

Reed Holloway: Mage. Younger brother of the triplet mages that helped found Avalon—Iris, Dahlia, and Violet Holloway. Lives in Avalon.

Thomas Bettencourt: Half vampire, half wolf shifter. Gifted with magic over technology. Leader of the Bettencourt vampire coven. Mated with Sage Montgomery. Lives in Avalon.

Sage Montgomery: Half wolf shifter, half vampire. Alpha of the Montgomery wolf pack. Mated with Thomas Bettencourt. Lives part time in Avalon, and part time in Hollywood Hills, California with the Montgomery pack.

Rosella: Vampire. Gifted with future sight. Lives in the Haven—the peaceful, neutral vampire kingdom in West India.

Amber Devereux: Witch. Torrence's mother. Lives in the Devereux mansion in Beverly Hills, California.

Chosen champions for this year's Faerie Games (all are half-blood fae who live in the Otherworld):

Antonia: Chosen champion of Apollo, the god of archery and music. Perfect aim.

Bridget: Chosen champion of Minerva, the goddess of war strategy. Future sight magic. Killed by Selena in the second week of the Faerie Games.

Cassia: Chosen champion of Ceres, the goddess of agriculture. Earth magic.

Cillian: Chosen champion of Pluto, the god of the Underworld. Metal magic.

Emmet: Chosen champion of Mercury, the messenger god. Air magic.

Felix: Chosen champion of Venus, the goddess of love. Seduction magic.

Molly: Chosen champion of Diana, the goddess of hunting. Animal shifting magic. Killed by Octavia in the first week of the Faerie Games.

Octavia: Chosen champion of Neptune, the god of the sea. Water magic.

Pierce: Chosen champion of Vulcan, the god of fire. Fire magic.

Gods we've met so far:

Bacchus: God of wine and celebration. He hosts the Faerie Games.

Juno: Queen of the gods, and the goddess of marriage and family. Juno creates the rules of the Faerie Games.

Vesta: Goddess of the hearth. She lives in the villa with the chosen champions and acts as a neutral mother figure to them.

WHERE WE LAST LEFT EVERYONE:

Selena, Julian, and Bridget faced off in the arena. Bridget tried to kill Julian, but Selena killed Bridget before she could harm him. Right before dying, Bridget revealed to Selena that Julian is Selena's soulmate.

King Devin—king of the violent vampire kingdom, The Tower—sent Torrence, Reed, Sage, and Thomas on a quest to find four mythical objects. If they bring him the objects, he'll tell them how to get to the Otherworld so they can rescue Selena.

Who will win the next Emperor of the Villa competition? Will Torrence and her group succeed in locating the mythical objects? And will Selena tell Julian that they're soulmates?

Turn the page to find out...

SELENA

"WELCOME to the third Emperor of the Villa competition!" a hologram of Bacchus said from the gold, basketball-sized orb floating in front of me. "This one's going to be a classic. A chariot race!"

I'd figured as much, since I was standing in the driver's seat of a gold chariot, holding the reins to control the four white horses connected to it. There was an ominous box of weapons in the area in front of my feet. And of course, I wore my personalized fighting outfit—a short, light blue dress with gladiator shoes that wrapped up to my knees.

The chariot was at the start of a straight dirt path around fifty feet wide, surrounded by grassy plains as far as the eye could see. There were no other champions

—no other *people*—anywhere. Just me, the horses, and Bacchus's annoying hologram.

"Each champion except our outgoing Empress of the Week, Octavia, is at the start of a road," Bacchus continued. "The roads are like the spokes of a wheel. They lead to the center, where the golden emperor wreath awaits. On my go, the champions will race down their road, facing separate—but identical—speed bumps along the way. The champion who gets the wreath will become this week's Emperor of the Villa!"

I gripped the reins tighter. *That sounds simple enough.*

"But there's a catch." Bacchus's playful eyes turned serious. "The champions cannot cross over the lines of their paths onto the grass. If they do, they'll be eliminated from the competition, and will lose their chance to become Emperor of the Week."

The road was *wide*. Staying on it shouldn't be a problem. The only wild card was the horses. I'd have to keep them in control so they wouldn't run out onto the grass.

Little jolts of lightning should do the trick.

I didn't like the idea of using my magic like a whip on animals. But after the last two disastrous weeks, I needed to win this competition. I'd do whatever it took to do that.

"Good luck, Champions!" Bacchus said. "On my mark, get set, GO!"

The horses took off.

I stumbled, nearly tumbling off the back of the chariot. But since I was holding tight onto the reins, I pulled myself forward, steadied myself, and stayed center.

The wind whipped past my face as I flew down the path. The air smelled like freshly cut grass and sweet flowers. And much to my delight, the horses ran perfectly straight. I barely had to do a thing.

Hopefully that meant the gods were favoring me in this competition.

After only a few minutes, I saw a looming creature blocking the path ahead. An ugly, two-headed dog that was slightly smaller than the horses. It looked like Cerberus's younger brother, but with one head missing.

"Whoa!" I yanked back on the reins. The horses slowed, stopping when we were ten feet away from the hideous, salivating dog.

That was close.

"Stay," I told the horses, hoping they'd understand.

One in the front bobbed its head up and down, which I took as a yes.

I grabbed the sword at my feet, hopped off the chariot, and put myself between the horses and the dog. My objective was clear. Take down the dog so I could continue on my way.

Slicing off its heads should work.

I'd trained with a sword back on Avalon. There was no reason why I shouldn't be able to do this. But it was still comforting to know that since this was an Emperor of the Villa competition, the fight wasn't to the death. The gods had spelled the monsters so they'd only knock us out—not kill us.

Still, being knocked out meant being knocked out of the competition. I couldn't afford to have that happen.

"Come at me, Cerberus Junior." I balanced on the balls of my feet and bounced my knees, holding my sword at the ready. "Show me what you've got."

Its eyes glowed yellow, and it bared its sharp teeth.

Then it pounced, its mouths wide and ready to chomp.

I did what any sane person would do—I rolled to the side to get out of the way. I'd be no good in the competition if this beast ripped my arms off. But I quickly bounced back onto my feet, spun around, and swung my sword straight down at its body.

The creature was fast, so I missed its body and sliced off its tail instead.

One head whimpered. The other howled. The dog prowled forward, and I backed up, keeping a safe amount of space between us.

Suddenly, it pounced again, and I rolled to the side—again. The edge of the path flashed in the corner of my eye. I jumped to my feet, steadying myself so I didn't cross over into the grass.

That was close.

I spun to face the dog, but it was no longer looking at me.

It was staring down my horses.

No. I sprinted forward, positioning myself between my horses and the dog.

The dog's eyes glowed brighter. It pawed at the ground, dirt coming up in little puffs under its claws.

My heart raced, panic setting in. The dog was on the offense, and I was barely keeping up the defense.

It needed to be the other way around. And if I wanted to intimidate this monster, I had to think like a dog—not like a half-blood fae, or Jupiter's chosen champion, or a faulty witch with no magic.

Think, I told myself, taking deep breaths to calm down. *I've seen wolves fight on Avalon. How do they state their dominance?*

They stood as straight as possible, held each other's gazes, and circled slowly around each other.

Since the dog was physically stronger than me, I had a better chance at beating it from afar.

So I dropped the sword and held my arms up so my palms faced each other, electricity buzzing in my hands.

Come on, lightning. It's time for you to do your thing.

Holding the dog's eyes was difficult, since it had four instead of two. So I did my best, focusing on the eyes on the inside of its faces. It seemed to work.

I stepped forward. The dog matched my step, shortening the space between us. Then I took two more steps, and it did the same.

There was only about ten feet between us.

My lightning sizzled and popped. But even though I was in danger, the closer I got to the dog, my magic didn't surface. No bolts between my palms, and certainly no bolts from the sky.

Frustration rose in me, but still, nothing.

Not wanting to get any closer to the dog without at least a *little* bit of magic between my hands, I started circling it. It mirrored my steps.

I focused on my magic, trying to push out the electricity flowing inside of me. I'd done it before. Why couldn't I do it now?

I clenched my teeth, beads of sweat collecting on my brow as I put everything I could into trying to harness my lightning.

Suddenly, the dog spun and leaped at my horses.

"NO!" I screamed, but it was too late.

The dog's jaws wrapped around the two front horses' necks. Blood spurted out of their veins and stained their white coats red. The dog kept its jaws locked down, lapping the blood with its tongues.

The horses struggled to free themselves, but it was no use. Their big eyes widened as they stared outward, frightened as the life drained out of their bodies.

There was so much blood.

An image flashed in my mind of yesterday, when Bridget's blood had coated my hands.

Anger crackled through me, I raised my hands, and lightning burst out of each palm.

It joined together and struck the dog in the center of its back.

The dog froze, seizing as I kept my hold on the lightning. But its jaws were still around the horses' necks. I pushed more of my magic into the bolts, until finally, the dog collapsed onto the ground.

The bodies of the horses collapsed with it.

I ran to grab my sword, hurried back, and cut the reins that held the front two horses to the chariot. Then I jumped back on.

"It's just the three of us now," I told the remaining two horses. I glanced down at the bloody mess in front of us, my heart breaking at the sight of the beautiful creatures lying in puddles of their own blood. "Don't look at them," I said to myself as much as to the two living horses, gripping the reins and trying to direct them around the mess.

One of them let out a sad neigh. The other lowered its neck and nudged one of the fallen horses with its nose. As it did, the dog twitched.

I looked closer, positive I'd imagined it. Sure enough, there was another twitch.

How's it recovering so quickly?

I didn't know. But I needed to get out of there, pronto.

"Come on." I zapped a bit of electricity through the reins—not enough to hurt the horses, but enough to get their attention. "Let's go."

One more zap, and then, we were off.

2

SELENA

THE HORSES PULLED the chariot slower than they had before, since there were two of them instead of four. But still, we were moving.

I just had to hope that the other champions took longer to fight the two-headed dog.

We traveled for ten minutes before another monster appeared ahead. I pulled on the reins to slow the horses down. They stopped sooner than they had for the dog. They must have learned their lesson.

The monstrosity in front of me had the head of a lion, with curved goat horns coming out of its forehead, the body of an antelope, and a metallic tail with a triangular point. It looked like it had been created by Dr. Frankenstein. It was smaller than the two-headed dog— it was closer to my size—but it looked twice as lethal.

I glanced at the weapons at my feet. Which one would be best against this thing?

Electricity surged under my skin, answering the question for me.

My magic has more power than all those weapons combined.

Decision made, I hopped out of the chariot empty handed. A bolt of lightning buzzed between my hands as I marched toward the monster. It was like my magic had been turned on during the fight with the dog, and now it didn't want to turn off.

Fine by me.

The creature dug its front hooves into the ground and lowered its head, pointing its horns at me.

Challenge accepted.

I continued forward, the air whipping around me as I gathered more magic. Once it felt like it was about to explode out of me, I flung out my hands and shot the bolt toward the creature.

Its tail zipped through the air, and the triangular point connected with the lightning, reflecting it off like a mirror.

The lightning bounced back and struck the ground a few feet away from me. I jumped at the sudden crack.

Crap.

The gods must have created this hodgepodge of a monster to throw me off.

They didn't want me to do well in this competition. I clenched my fists, furious at them for purposefully stacking this fight against me.

But the creature only had one tail. I just needed to attack with two bolts instead of one.

Fueled with anger, I stormed forward, power rushing through me as I blasted the creature with two identical, separate bolts of lightning.

Its tail whizzed around in a blur, deflecting both of them seemingly at once.

I stopped in place. Heart pounding, I glanced back at the chariot. It was time to get a weapon.

But which one?

Before I could decide, the monster threw itself on top of me and pinned me to the ground. It was only thanks to quick reflexes that I grabbed its neck to hold it off. Its jaws got closer and closer, its breath hot in my face as it descended toward my neck. Its eyes glowed with determination, and it chomped its teeth, inches away from crushing my neck in its jaws.

It was going to behead me.

The god of healing, Vejovis, had powerful magic. But once someone died, there was no coming back.

It can't be trying to kill me, I reminded myself as I

stared up into its murderous eyes. *The gods cast a spell on the monsters. They can't kill us.*

I pushed harder, trying to get it off of me. But it kept descending downward.

It wasn't stopping. It *was* trying to kill me. The golden orbs buzzed behind it, recording every moment. I thought I saw the flicker of a face in one of them, and hope of rescue bloomed in my chest. But when I looked again, the face was gone—if it had even been there at all.

I refused to let this be the end. Bridget had sacrificed herself for me, and I wanted to learn why. I still hadn't told Julian that we were soulmates. And the Nephilim army was on its way to save me—I knew it in my heart.

I was going to stay alive. I was going to get home to Avalon, and I was going to bring Julian and Cassia back with me.

Electricity snapped and popped within me, growing stronger as the monster closed in. Once my lightning built up to maximum voltage, I screamed and forced the most powerful jolt I'd created yet into the monster.

Its eyes glowed bright, its body lighting up as my magic filled its system. Its head arched to the sky and it spasmed a few times. The light flickered out, and the monster rolled onto the ground beside me, dead.

At least I *thought* it was dead. It hadn't disintegrated,

so there was no way to know for sure. And I wasn't staying long enough to find out.

So I brushed the dirt off my dress, ran to the chariot, and took off without looking back.

There was one more monster in my path—a hideous woman with the body of a bird. She swooped down from the sky, dug her talons into my shoulders, and flew me up out of the chariot. The horses stopped, confused.

The monster was trying to drag me off the boundary of the path.

No way was I letting that happen. As Jupiter's chosen champion, the sky was *my* domain.

As the ground got farther away, fury surged through me, and wind whipped across my face. My magic was a living thing, and I relished its power.

One lightning strike perfectly aimed between her shoulder bones, and her talons released me.

I hurtled down to the ground, bending my knees and rolling into the fall. Pain reverberated through me, but I'd been trained in how to fall properly. There were no broken bones.

I sat up and saw that I was only a few feet away from the edge of the path. Another close call. The bird monster had landed on the grass, and all of her feathers had molted off.

She didn't look scary now that she was bald.

But time was of the essence. As much as I wanted to check to see if my bolt had killed her, I couldn't afford to lose even a minute.

So I ran back to the chariot, took off, and left her behind in my dust.

3

SELENA

AFTER A FEW MORE MINUTES, the plain turned into rolling hills. The path curved around them so I couldn't see far ahead. As I continued, the path grew more and more narrow, like a funnel. Finally, two identical hills came into view, the path leading straight through the middle of it.

The center of the wheel. And Bacchus still hadn't announced the winner. Which meant no one had gotten the wreath yet.

I could still win this competition.

My chariot flew through the path between the hills, and I was right. All eight paths converged into a circular area about half the size of the fighting ring in the Coliseum.

There was a giant tree in the center. The wreath sat

on top of it. But a green magical boundary circled around the tree, with only one gap to enter.

A giant, hideous snake guarded the entrance. Spikes protruded from the back of its neck, going all the way down to its tail. Its eyes glowed blue, although it wasn't looking at me.

It was looking at Cillian. Pluto's champion had raised all the metal from the ground—gold, silver, bronze, and the like—and was seconds away from hurling it at the snake. But the snake's eyes flashed yellow, Cillian's eyes flashed the same yellow, and the metal crashed to the ground. He collapsed into an unconscious heap on the dirt.

Cillian's impulsive, I realized. *That's his weakness.*

Julian and Pierce were off to the side, moving in a blur as they faced off. Julian wielded two swords, and Pierce threw balls of fire. They moved so fast that it was impossible to tell who was ahead in the fight. But then Pierce's fire attacks slowed down. He was still fighting, but Julian must have swiped him with one of his swords.

Antonia stood on the opposite side of the arena. She was using her bow to shoot arrows at the snake, but her head was turned so she wasn't looking at it. Unsurprisingly, her aim was off. Most of the arrows missed. A few hit the snake, but they either bounced off the lethal-looking spikes or hit the body. The body shots made the snake open its mouth and hiss at her, showing off its venomous fangs.

"Don't look it in the eyes!" Julian screamed while holding off Pierce's attacks.

"Got it!" I replied, although I'd already figured that out after watching Cillian go down.

Suddenly, something flew at me and hit me in the leg. I screamed and glanced down at the arrow sticking out above my kneecap.

Antonia. She was no longer aiming at the basilisk.

She'd decided to take me out first.

Instinct told me to yank out the arrow. But then I'd lose blood. It hurt like hell, but I needed to leave it where it was until the competition was over.

Another arrow struck above my other knee. I screamed and stumbled back, falling to the ground on my butt.

I pushed up on my hands and tried standing up. But my legs refused to hold up my body. I grunted and fell right back down.

Antonia held her bow at the ready, about to shoot another arrow.

This time, I was ready.

I raised my hands and shot out bolts of lightning, taking down each arrow like I'd taken out the bunches of grapes during the first arena fight to the death. I felt like I could hold her off forever.

But if any other champions arrived at the center of the wheel, I was a sitting duck. I needed to take out Antonia—not just her arrows. And I needed to do it now.

Knock her out. Don't kill her.

I took a deep breath. Bryan and Finn had trained me to use this type of control.

I could do it.

I held off her arrows with one hand and gathered electricity with another. Once I had enough—but not *too* much—I threw the bolt of lightning straight at her stomach.

She seized and fell backward, as straight as a board. Her head smacked to the ground.

I stared at her, holding my breath. Bound to the ground, I couldn't run over to check her pulse to make sure she was still alive.

But Juno hadn't appeared to take me out for breaking the no killing rule.

Antonia was still alive.

My muscles relaxed, and I could breathe again. But the comfort only lasted for a second.

Because there was still the issue of the giant snake.

Thank God the snake was only guarding the gate and wasn't going on the offensive.

Otherwise, I'd have been toast already.

I glanced over my shoulder at Julian and Pierce. Julian took another swing—an attempt to slice off Pierce's arm. But Pierce moved quickly enough that it created a nasty gash instead of removing his arm completely.

I needed to take care of the snake, and I needed to do it quickly. Because who knew when any of the other champions would come riding down their path.

Julian or I needed to get the wreath before that could happen.

It needs to be Julian, I realized. *With my legs like this, I can't climb the tree to get the wreath.*

I glanced over to see if he was still ahead in his fight with Pierce. He was.

Looking down to avoid looking the snake in the eyes, I dug deep within myself and gathered as much magic as I could.

My entire body lit up, glowing with electricity. I *was* electricity, and the electricity was me.

Looking at the snake's body instead of its eyes, I gathered my magic into two lethal balls in my hands. They glowed so brightly that I couldn't look straight at them.

I held my palms forward and pushed.

The bolts joined together mid-air, striking the snake where its heart should be. I pushed more magic into the bolt to keep it in place. The snake shook and seized, although I could only tell from looking at its body, since I was avoiding his eyes.

"I can't hold it much longer," I screamed, unable to look away from the snake because I didn't want to lose my hold on it. "You have to get the wreath NOW!"

In the corner of my eye, I saw someone run past the snake and through the gate. But with the bright light of the lightning in front of me—nearly blinding me—I couldn't tell if it was Julian or Pierce.

Please be Julian.

"We have our new Emperor of the Villa!" Bacchus's voice boomed through the air.

I dropped hold of my lightning and fell onto my back. My knees throbbed in agony, and the world spun around me as I stared up at the puffy white clouds. My eyes wanted to close so I could float away to an unconscious place free of pain.

But I fought it. I needed to know who won.

"Congratulations Julian, the chosen champion of Mars!" Bacchus said.

Relief coursed through me, I relaxed into the ground, and the darkness pulled me under.

4

SELENA

WHEN I'D WOKEN up in the villa's healing chamber, my kneecaps were good as new.

Now, we were gathered around the table for Julian's celebration banquet. Cassia, Felix, and I sat by his sides.

Octavia and her lackeys were relegated to the far end.

"Did the chimera try to kill any of you back there?" I asked after the roasted pig was served.

That was what I'd learned the ugly, Frankenstein monster was called. A chimera.

Octavia rolled her eyes. "And the paranoia has set in," she said. "It figures you'd be the first to succumb."

"What do you mean by that?"

"The monsters don't try to kill us in the Emperor of the Villa competitions." She sneered. "The gods make sure of it. But being locked in a villa together affects most people's minds. It makes them moody, unable to think straight, and paranoid. It's basic psychology. The weaker minded are the first to succumb."

I placed my utensils down and held her gaze. "The chimera was going straight for my neck," I said. "I didn't imagine it."

"Mine went for my extremities," Cassia piped in. "Not my neck."

The others said the same.

"See?" Octavia said. "It wasn't trying to rip your head off. It's just the paranoia talking." She smiled sweetly and took a delicate bite of meat.

I said nothing more. But I knew what I saw. The chimera was definitely going for my neck.

But I wasn't the only one watching, I reminded myself. *The entire Otherworld was watching through the orbs.*

If the chimera was truly trying to kill me, the gods would have stopped it. They didn't want us taken out of the Games that way. They wanted us to kill each other in the arena.

Maybe I *was* being paranoid.

But I ate the rest of my meal in silence, since I'd never admit to Octavia that she might be right.

Everyone but myself, Cassia, Felix, and Julian left the dining room the moment the meal was over.

Julian turned to me, and my heart raced when his eyes met mine. "I need to talk to you," he said.

"What's up?" I tried to sound as casual as possible.

"Not here." He glanced down the hall that led to the stairs. "In my suite."

"You two go ahead." Felix stood up and placed his hand on Cassia's shoulder. "The aurora is supposed to be brighter than normal tonight. I was hoping Cassia and I might watch it together."

Her cheeks flushed, even more when she looked up to him and met his eyes. "I'd love that," she said.

"I'm glad." He lifted his hand from her shoulder and held it out to her, helping her out of her chair. His hand still in hers, he turned slightly to Julian. "Congrats on the win, brother," he said.

Julian bristled when Felix called him brother, although Felix and Cassia all but floated out of the dining room before he could respond.

"Shall we?" Julian motioned to the hall that led to the stairs.

I nodded and followed his lead, the butterflies in my stomach so intense that I could barely stay steady as I walked.

This would be our first time alone together since I

saw his clover birthmark that matched mine. I needed to tell him. But how?

Don't be nervous, I told myself as we walked up the stairs. Each step took so much effort that I felt like I was climbing Everest. *He's your soulmate. And he deserves to know.*

5

SELENA

JULIAN LOUNGED ON THE BED, as comfortable as ever.

I sat on one of the armchairs facing him, sitting as straight as a board.

He was talking about the game—about his plans for what he was going to do for the week. I wasn't hearing a word he was saying.

What if he's disappointed to be my soulmate?

He'd pushed me away when we'd kissed last week. It was one of the most humiliating moments of my life.

He won't be disappointed, another part of my mind thought. *That's not how the soulmate bond works. He has to feel the same draw to me that I feel toward him. He just has to.*

But the way he'd looked at me after he pushed me away wouldn't leave my mind. Like I disgusted him.

How could my soulmate feel that way about me? Could our matching birthmarks be a fluke? Could there be a small difference between them—something so small that I wouldn't see it until we studied them next to each other?

"Selena." He snapped his fingers, bringing me back into focus. "Are you hearing a word I'm saying?"

"Sorry." I shook my head to clear my thoughts. "I just have a lot on my mind."

His expression softened, and he patted the place on the bed next to him. "Want to talk about it?"

Yes.

No.

I'm not ready for this.

But when would be a better time? When would there *ever* be a good time to tell him that we were soulmates playing in a game where only one of us was supposed to come out alive?

I needed to do it now.

So I stood up, my feet concrete bricks as I made my way over to him. I sat next to him and leaned back into the comfortable pillows. Being so close to him felt right. And the way he was looking at me—so understanding, so patient—made me want to spill my heart to him.

"Thank you," he said seriously. "For trusting me to get the wreath."

"My kneecaps were busted." I chuckled in an unsuccessful attempt to lessen the intensity between us. "I had no choice."

"You always have a choice," he said. "And you chose to trust that I'd protect you."

"I have no choice but to trust you," I said.

"What do you mean by that?"

I swallowed and lowered my hand to the top of my skirt. Then I pulled it down slightly to reveal the clover birthmark on my left hipbone. I was so worried about how he'd react that I couldn't look up at him. "I have no choice because you're my soulmate."

The next thing I knew, Julian's fingers touched my chin, forcing my eyes up to meet his. Then his lips were on mine, moving slowly and gently. I melted into him. This kiss was different than the others—softer and more loving. Sparks of electricity ignited every part of my body, yet at the same time, I felt calmer than I'd felt since Bridget revealed his birthmark to me.

I no longer had to pretend that the connection between us was wrong or in my imagination. From the way he was kissing me, I knew he felt it, too.

My heart would forever belong to Julian, and his would forever belong to me.

Eventually we pulled back, our foreheads resting against each other's before I pulled away to look up at him. His pupils were dilated, and he stared down at me in wonder.

"I guess you're not disappointed?" I asked.

"Disappointed?" he repeated, shocked. "I haven't been able to stop thinking about you since the moment I saw you. I thought I was going crazy. I thought I was betraying my family by the pull I felt to protect you in the Games—with the need to keep you safe no matter what. Now it all makes sense."

"But last week, in the backyard…" I lowered my eyes again, barely able to say it. "You pushed me away."

"Look at me," he said, and I did. The fierceness in his eyes took my breath away. "I was scared. The only other person I've ever felt scared for is my sister. So when I felt that way for you, I panicked. I've been beating myself up about it since it happened. The look on your face—the hurt that I caused you—it hasn't left my mind." He kissed the sensitive spot below one of my ears, and then the other. I shivered with pleasure at his touch. "Just tell me what to do to make it up to you," he said. "Anything, and I'll do it."

With him so close to me, my body took over, and we were kissing again. We fell into the pillows, and I pressed myself against him. The hardness under his breeches slipped between my thighs, and a soft moan escaped my lips, a spot deep in my stomach throbbing with the need for more.

But there was sadness in the kiss. And as much as I tried to ignore it—as much as I tried to lose myself in what should have been a perfect moment—I couldn't.

I buried my face in his shoulder, my body pulsing with need. He groaned, and I knew he was struggling to control himself, too.

"Selena," he murmured, burying his fingers in my hair. "You have no idea what you're doing to me."

"If it's anything close to what you're doing to me, then trust me, I do." I wiggled my hips, although I somehow managed to stop. "But I've never been with anyone like this before. And the Games… the two of us… I don't want the darkness of death hanging over us." I paused, realizing I wasn't making any sense. I couldn't form words when my body was begging for the release it so desperately needed.

I closed my eyes and forced myself to be still. When I finally opened them, I saw he was doing the same.

I traced a finger over his perfect cheekbone, and the tension in his face relaxed. No matter what happened in the future, I'd never forget this moment.

He opened his eyes again, looking more patient than I'd expected. "Tell me what you need." He sat up, pulled me onto his lap, and brushed soft kisses along my neck.

I whimpered, leaning my head back in pleasure as my last bit of control vanished. "I'm yours. Every single part of me—it's yours."

"I want you." I ground my hips against his as the mounting need took over. "*Now.*"

"We're waiting until you're ready," he said firmly. "But until then…" He locked his gaze with mine, and his hand traveled under my skirt, past my undergarment, and between my thighs. When he felt the wetness there, he let out a low growl and slipped his fingers inside me.

I gasped as my core exploded with warmth, and I wrapped my arms around his neck, rocking my hips until I came apart in his hand. He groaned with need, and I reached inside his breeches to take his hardness in my palm. He murmured my name as I caressed him, and with his fingers still inside me, we peaked together.

I sank into him and rested my head on his shoulder. "I want you *forever*," I said, pulling back to look into his eyes. "But with the Games, we don't have forever. If we don't stop them, one or both of us will die. If not this week, then maybe the week after that, or the one after that."

He ran his fingers through my tangled hair. "What do you mean, 'stop them?'" he said, as if the words themselves were blasphemy. "The Games have been happening for centuries. We can't stop them."

I sighed and fell back into the pillows, since ideas about how to stop the Games were all I'd been thinking about since seeing Julian's soulmate mark. He walked to the wardrobe to change, and then collapsed next to me.

The golden orbs floated above us, recording our every move.

The entire Otherworld had just watched us lose ourselves in each other.

But I didn't regret it. Because the more the fae saw the intensity of our soulmate bond, the more they might rally in our favor.

"There have never been soulmates in the Games before, right?" I finally asked.

"Right."

"Is there an actual *rule* regarding soulmates in the Games?"

"Not that I know of." He pressed his lips together, thinking. "Half-blood soulmates are so rare that I doubt Juno thought a rule would be necessary."

"So we can ask to be excused from the Games," I said quickly. "The fae know how strong the soulmate bond is. Surely not even they want to watch us go through this torture. And I know you're here for Vita, but like you said earlier, we're family now. Which means Vita's *my* sister, too. On Avalon, we want for nothing. Vita will have all the medicine she needs."

"Selena." He sat up and pressed his fingers to his temples. "Even if we can be excused from the Games—and that's a *big* if—it doesn't mean we'll be able to get to Avalon. At least not anytime soon. And by then…"

The unsaid part of the sentence lingered in the air.

By then, who knows what will have happened to Vita?

"The Nephilim army is coming for us," I said, sitting up as well. "My parents don't love royal titles, but my mother is the queen of Avalon. My father is the prince, which basically makes him king consort."

"Do you want me to start calling you Princess Selena?" He cracked a small smile, despite the direness of the situation.

"Please, don't," I said. "But the fact is, I *am* a princess. And Avalon's army will go to the ends of the Earth to get me home safely."

"I hope you're right," he said. "But right now, they're *not* here. We have to proceed as if they're not coming."

My heart dropped. Because as much as I wanted to have faith in the Nephilim army, I knew he was right.

"However, you're right about the lack of rules regarding soulmates," he said. "We can talk to Vesta to see if anything can be done."

"But your sister…" I trailed.

"I won't lose her," he said. "But I also won't lose you.

32

I'm going to keep *both* of you safe. And the first step toward doing that is to get us out of here."

"So you think it's possible?"

"We won't know until we ask." He pulled me off the bed, and we walked together toward the hearth. "Vesta," he said, strong and confident. "We need to speak with you."

Flames burst in the hearth, and Vesta stepped through. She wore the same flowing orange dress as always. "Julian and Selena," she said, clasping her hands in front of herself and giving us a warm smile. "I was wondering when I'd finally hear from you."

6

SELENA

As MUCH AS I wanted to stay in Julian's suite that night, I forced myself to go back down to the bedroom I shared with the other girls. It was bad enough that they already knew Julian, Cassia, and I were in an alliance. If they knew Julian and I were soulmates? They'd come after us in a heartbeat. Which meant we had to keep our soulmate bond secret from everyone—including Cassia and Felix.

The next day, it didn't take long for Felix to make his way up to Julian's suite. He lounged on the couch, while Julian and I were on the bed. I made sure not to sit *too* close to Julian, even though every part of my body was urging me closer to him.

"Our plan's good to go?" Felix asked.

"Yep," Julian said. "You, Octavia, and Cillian will be heading to the arena this week."

"Good." Hate filled Felix's eyes. "Pretending that I like Octavia…" He shuddered. "She's a sour person, and she tastes sour, too. It takes every effort not to flinch every time I touch her."

"I can't imagine," I said.

"I gotta do what I gotta do." He shrugged. "Even if that means wanting to kill her every time I kiss her."

I was glad Cassia wasn't there to hear the details about what we all suspected was going on between Felix and Octavia behind closed doors. But this was the first time Felix had voiced his disgust about Octavia—and it was the first time he'd made it clear that there was more than just flirting between them.

Has he touched Octavia the same way Julian touched me?

I glanced at Julian out of the corner of my eye, my cheeks heating at the memory of how intimate we were last night. Warmth throbbed below my stomach just from thinking about it. If Felix weren't there right now…

"It'll be immensely satisfying to watch Cillian take out Octavia." Felix crossed his legs and smirked. "She deserves what's coming for her."

I opened my mouth to say no one deserved to be

killed, but then closed it. Because Octavia was in a league of her own.

"Octavia needs to go," Julian agreed. "And I'm glad to see you're a man of your word. Thanks for volunteering for the arena this week."

"My pleasure," he said. "The four of us until the end, right?"

"Right." Julian's voice was firm.

I only nodded. Because by the time we were supposed to reach final four, I intended to be far away from the Otherworld.

"Speaking of the final four," Felix continued. "I had to leave Cassia down there with the sharks so I could check in with the two of you. I don't want to leave her there alone for any longer than I have to." He glanced at the door, looking truly worried.

"You really do care about her," I said "Don't you?"

"Cassia's special," he said. "She's too good-hearted for the Games. I might not have long with her, but while we're both still here, she deserves to be loved." He lowered his eyes, as if embarrassed for admitting his feelings. Then he stood up and walked to the door, turning to face us again when his hand was around the knob. "Anyway, I know you two lovebirds need your time alone—"

"It's not like that," I broke in, although the lie was less than convincing.

"Come on." Felix rolled his eyes. "I'm the chosen champion of Venus. I can smell your raging hormones from downstairs."

"We haven't…" I trailed off, since I had no intention of giving Felix the details.

"No judgment here." He held his hands up in innocence. "Releasing your stress is healthy. But as I was saying, it might not be a bad idea to go down there and mingle. Make some more connections with the other champions. You know the drill."

He left, and the moment the door shut, Julian and I closed the space between us. I didn't know who kissed who first, but soon I was laying flat on the bed, and his hard, muscular body was on top of mine.

"Felix is probably right," I managed to say in between kisses. "We should go down and mingle."

"We probably should." His lips were quickly on mine again, and neither of us made an effort to stop.

Our kisses grew more desperate, our bodies moving in perfect rhythm together. Stopping without a repeat of last night was going to be physically impossible.

Suddenly, heat flared across my skin. And it didn't come from inside of me.

Julian and I turned our heads simultaneously to look at the hearth.

Vesta stood in front of the blazing fireplace.

Next to her was the most impossibly beautiful woman I'd ever seen.

With long golden hair, a heart shaped face, and skin so perfect that it must have been air brushed, the woman was ethereal in a way that the most stunning movie stars could only dream about. Her white and gold dress showed off as much of her perfect figure as possible, but I had a feeling she'd be gorgeous even in a potato sack.

Julian was off of me in a flash, standing in front of the foot of the bed and straightening his clothes. I did the same.

The orbs that had been in the room a minute ago were gone.

"Pardon the interruption," Vesta said with a knowing smile. "But after our chat last night, there's someone I want you to meet."

The beautiful woman gave Vesta a haughty look and brought her hair over her shoulder. "I assume they've already figured out who I am." She looked at Julian, and then at me, with an expression that said we either got this right or she'd want nothing to do with us. "They always do."

There was only one person I knew who came close to matching her arrogance. And he'd only just left this room.

"You're Venus." I straightened my shoulders and held her gaze. "The goddess of love."

7

SELENA

"I KNEW you'd get it right," she said. "Especially since both of you have been marked by my own hand."

"You mean our soulmate marks?" I asked.

"Of course." She walked over to the couch and sat down, lounging with her legs out so she took up the entire thing. "It's entertaining to watch humans try—and usually fail—to find their soulmates. But I've always had a special place in my heart for the fae. Your magic, intelligence, and tenacity impress me. I want to see your kind find the happiness that only true love can bring. But with so many fae out there, and with lust oftentimes becoming a blinding distraction, finding your soulmate can be close to impossible. Thus, I created the soulmate mark. Brilliant, right?"

"Brilliant." Julian stood so straight and tense that I

knew it was taking his every effort not to rush toward Venus and strangle her swan-like neck.

"You're angry with me." Venus tilted her head coquettishly. "Why?"

"Why do you think?"

"It can't have anything to do with the soulmate I chose for you," she said. "Selena's beautiful. And that means a lot, coming from me."

I shifted uncomfortably. I'd been so uninterested in all the guys on Avalon that I'd never given my looks much thought. Other than Torrence—who didn't count, because as my best friend, she *had* to be nice about stuff like that—the only person who'd ever called me beautiful was Julian.

And now, apparently, Venus.

"Selena is the kindest, most loving, most beautiful person I've ever met." Julian wrapped his arm protectively around my waist, his words leaving me speechless. "The situation we're in is cruel, even by the standards of the gods."

"Is it, though?" Venus studied her manicured nails. "Would you rather have died—or have watched her die —without knowing what you are to each other?"

"You're enjoying this." Hatred for the beautiful goddess bloomed in my chest.

Venus shrugged, not answering one way or the other.

"Drop the act, Venus," Vesta said, harsher then I'd ever heard her speak before. "They don't need to be tortured any more than they already are."

"Fine." Venus huffed and propped herself up straighter. "I'll give it to you straight. Much like my fellow gods, I've always enjoyed the Games. But this…" She shook her head, looking sadly between Julian and me. "Soulmates are supposed to be together forever, or at least able to enjoy the time they have. Your situation crosses a line that I simply will not stand for."

Relief washed over me, and I leaned into Julian's embrace. "Does that mean you're creating a rule for the Games regarding soulmates?" I asked hopefully.

She pursed her perfectly pouty lips. "When Vesta came to me and explained your plight, my heart went out to you." She frowned and placed her hand on her chest. "It only felt right to deliver the news myself."

The relief from earlier vanished.

"What news?" Julian was on guard once again.

"Juno created the rules of the Games. She's the only one who can change them or add new ones," Venus said. "You're correct that there's no rule regarding soulmates. So I went to Juno and requested a new rule that soulmates should be allowed to be excused from the Games, if that's what they wish."

"And?" I bounced on my toes, unable to handle the

anticipation.

"She denied it," Venus said flatly.

I knew it was coming—I could tell by her tone. But despair crashed through me anyway, so heavy that I had to lean further into Julian to stop from falling over.

"Juno said the Games this year are particularly important, and that the two of you *must* stay in them," Venus continued. "I don't know how she knows that. I assume she's spoken with Minerva." She shrugged again. "I'm afraid all I can tell you is that new rules can be created at any time, and that you should always have faith in the gods."

I stared at her, speechless.

She was asking me to have faith in the gods who thought it was fun to gift half-bloods with their magic and watch them fight it out until only one of them remained alive.

No thanks.

"On that note, it's time I take my leave." Venus stood up and brushed invisible lint off her gown. "Come, Vesta. It's best they're left alone to digest this information together."

Vesta gave us a pitying look and shot her orange magic toward the hearth, lighting up the flames. Venus gave another flick of her golden hair, and then, she and Vesta disappeared into the fire.

8

SELENA

"THERE'S STILL THE NEPHILIM ARMY." I turned to Julian once the flames died out. "They'll save us before the Games' end, and we'll both get out of this alive. Cassia, too."

Julian's face was as hard as stone, and my heart dropped.

He doesn't believe me.

He reached for my hand and led me toward the couch, sitting down and coaxing me next to him. He sat there, still, for a few seconds. Finally, he turned to look at me, and I knew I was right. He didn't believe in the Nephilim army.

How could he? The Otherworld was cut off from Earth and Avalon. They didn't care what was happening in our realms. And even if the fae royals knew about the Nephilim army, why would they tell the half-bloods?

I braced myself for his inevitable admittance of disbelief in my people. In my *family*.

"I admire your optimism," he finally said. "And I believe you that the Nephilim army is strong."

"Do you really mean it? Or are you just saying that?"

"I mean it," he said. "Any kingdom that raises someone as fierce and brave as you must be a force to be reckoned with."

"They are." My heart warmed at the thought of my home and my family. I missed them so much that it hurt, every single day. "And thank you," I said, realizing I'd completely ignored his compliment. "I'm doing the best I can to stay strong."

"As you should," he said. "But the fae are strong, too. And time can work differently in the Otherworld than it does on Earth. I have no doubt that your family is searching for you. But if the fae are determined to keep you here, then time isn't going to be on your side."

"What?" I blinked, even though I'd heard him the first time. "*How* differently can time work between the Otherworld and Earth?"

"It varies." He spoke slowly, clearly worried about how I'd take what he was going to say next. "Time only moves differently when the fae will it to do so. The more fae involved, and the more magic they put into it, the larger the difference will be."

The world crumbled around me. "Could years have passed on Earth in the time I've been here?" I gripped the edge of the sofa to steady myself. *"Centuries?"*

"No." He reached for one of my hands, but even his touch didn't calm me. Not until I knew more. "Nothing like that. The largest difference I've ever heard of is one day on Earth passing for every week in the Otherworld. And that was only once."

"So that's the worst case scenario."

"Most likely," he said.

That didn't sound promising.

But I took a deep breath, since this was a lot of information to absorb at once. "So if we assume the worst case scenario, only a few days have passed on Earth. Which means the Nephilim army is still on their way."

"Maybe," he said. "Maybe not. Like I said, fae are strong. We're also tricky. They know your family will be doing everything they can to rescue you. They'll do anything they can to stop them—or at least, delay them. We have no way of knowing what kind of progress the Nephilim army is making. All we can do is what we're already doing—take this one week at a time."

"And then what?" I asked. "Do what Venus said and

have faith in the gods? Because the gods haven't given me much to have faith in."

"The gods are far from infallible," he said. "But Vesta has never brought another god into the villa during the Games. What just happened with Venus dropping by is unheard of."

"The orbs disappeared when she arrived," I reminded him, glancing at the orbs hovering around us now. It amazed me how used to them I'd gotten since that first week in the Games. "No one saw her. For all we know, anyone listening to us right now will think we're lying. Or maybe the orbs aren't broadcasting this conversation at all."

"Maybe," he said. "But Venus said that this year's games are important, and that we *must* stay in them. It's too similar to what Bridget told us before the arena fight to be a coincidence."

I nodded, since Bridget's words hadn't left my mind.

You need to live. The fate of the world depends on it.

"Before she died, Bridget made sure I saw your soul-mate mark," I said, speaking faster now that it felt like we were onto something. "There has to be a reason why. If she's right, and everything happening now is bigger than the Games, it means we were placed in this position for a reason. So there has to be something we can do from here—something to create change. Something to make it so more than one of us makes it out of the Games." I clasped his hands, as if holding onto them tightly could make it true.

"Perhaps," he said. "But until we figure out what that thing is, we need to stay alive."

"Agreed." Confidence rose in my chest at the small bit of hope. "So let's go downstairs, mingle with the other players, and get as many of them in our corner as possible."

9

TORRENCE

REED, Sage, Thomas, and I teleported to my family's home—the Devereux mansion—after leaving the Tower. We caught my mom up on everything that had happened since Selena's disappearance. She was worried for my safety on the mission, but it wasn't her place to tell me not to serve the Earth Angel. So she'd allowed us to look around the library in our basement.

"The mages in Mystica have excellent libraries," Reed said when he saw the multiple floors of sprawling wooden shelves. "But I must say, your family's archives are quite impressive."

I stopped walking and glared at him. "You're using 'quite' in the British sense, aren't you?" I asked.

Which would mean he *didn't* find the archives impressive.

"Partly." He smirked. "But I truly didn't expect much when you said we might be able to find information about the objects King Devin wants in here. Now, we may have a chance. Even if that chance is small."

"If the archives in Mystica are so great, why don't you bring us there instead?" I challenged.

"Because the archives in Mystica only chronicle our own history." He brushed off my question like the answer was obvious. "The problems on Earth never worried us—until you let that Hell Gate be opened so the demons could escape into your unprepared realm full of weak, clueless humans."

Sage spun around, her wolfish eyes flashing with anger. "We didn't *let* the Hell Gate be opened," she growled. "We fought a war while the mages were frolicking around on Mystica—or whatever it is you do there. Just be glad we closed it. And quickly, I might add."

Thomas stepped to her side and placed a hand on her shoulder, keeping his eyes on Reed. "As I'm sure you've seen, Earth has a plentiful amount of supernaturals fighting the demons, while ensuring that the humans remain clueless and calm," he said. "We've got this. After all, we don't want the demons leaking into Mystica, no matter how *prepared* you all might be."

Reed shrugged and walked past us to explore the library.

Sage, Thomas, and I shared a *look*.

We might have been prophesied to work with Reed to rescue Selena, but that didn't mean we had to like him.

"Torrence?" Thomas looked to me, ignoring Reed. "I'm guessing you have an idea where we should start?"

"I do." I smiled, breathed in the welcoming smell of books, and headed toward an aisle as far away from the one Reed had wandered off to as possible. "Follow me."

I slammed down the cover of what felt like the millionth book I was looking through. "Nothing," I said, pushing it to the end of the table.

The four of us were sitting around a large table, scanning through the books we'd pulled from the shelves. It was so late at night—or early in the morning, depending on how you looked at it—that my eyes hurt.

"We've been at this forever." Sage tossed the book she was holding into one of the many large reject piles. "How have we found *nothing*?"

Reed just whistled and continued flipping through the book on his lap.

Arrogant, obnoxious mage.

I rested my elbows on the table and rubbed my temples. "There has to be something," I said. "Maybe we're just not looking hard enough."

"We're looking pretty hard," Thomas said. "I already know the digital database of the Bettencourt archives doesn't have what we need. And while the Devereux archives are said to be some of the best in the world, perhaps the Haven archives has texts that yours doesn't."

I closed my eyes and thought harder. My family's library was *not* about to be outshined by the Haven. Our archives were supposedly linked with the souls of the witches in our circle. I should have been able to do this.

What am I missing?

Suddenly, something crashed in the far corner of the library.

My eyes snapped open, and I looked at where the sound had come from.

"The children's section." I pushed up from my chair and hurried in that direction. The others followed.

First, I went to the children's non-fiction section. We'd already checked those shelves, but maybe we'd missed something.

Everything there was the same. So I ventured into the aisle we hadn't looked at before. The children's *fiction* section.

An entire section of large, hardback books had fallen into the center of the aisle.

I rushed toward them and kneeled down to check them out. The others did the same, so we were gathered around the books like we were sitting around a campfire.

All of the books were by the same author. A woman I'd never heard of named Eloise D'Airoldi.

Tales of Norse Myths.
Tales of Arthurian Myths.
Tales of Roman Myths.
Tales of Christian Myths.
Tales of Greek Myths.
Tales of Jewish Myths.
Tales of Egyptian Myths.

And more. There must have been at least twenty of them in all.

I snatched the one on Greek myths and opened it to the dedication page.

"To those who see the truth—that all the stories are real," I read aloud.

"That's in mine, too." Sage held up the book about Christianity.

Thomas and Reed confirmed it was in theirs as well. A glance at the first pages in all the other books revealed identical dedications.

The stories inside were written for children, complete with detailed illustrations. We took a closer look through the legends we were the most familiar with—Arthurian, Christian, and Jewish. They were startlingly accurate.

"All of the stories are real," I repeated the line from the dedication. "Greek, Roman, Egyptian… all of it. Just like King Devin said."

"That's what this author seems to believe," Sage agreed.

"I don't know why you're all so shocked," Reed said. "You've seen the Holy Grail and Excalibur. You live on the actual island of Avalon." He looked pointedly at the book on Arthurian myths. "You've seen demons from Hell. You've seen Nephilim, prophets, and according to the Earth Angel and Prince Jacen, a troll. Why should any of the stories chronicled throughout your history be more or less real than the others?"

His words shocked us into silence. I didn't think I'd ever heard Reed say that many words in a row, well… ever.

"I don't know." I shrugged. "We've always been taught that the most ancient ones are only myths."

"School doesn't teach you everything," he said simply.

I gripped the edges of the book I was holding, hating that I couldn't tell him he was wrong.

"Whether these stories are real or not, the books wanted to be found." Thomas glanced at me with respect. "So, let's bring them over to the table. Because we have research to do."

10

SELENA

"WELCOME to the third arena fight of the Faerie Games!" Bacchus said from his chariot flown by jaguars, his voice booming through the Coliseum. "Who's ready to see the chosen champions of Neptune, Venus, and Pluto face off to the death?"

The crowd erupted into raucous applause.

The inside of the arena was standing room only. People were also gathered outside the Coliseum, watching on the orbs in the streets.

The center of the arena was covered with grass, tiny hills, and miniature trees. Wild animals prowled in circles, staring at each other like they were ready to pounce.

"See the animals down there?" Bacchus pointed his scepter down toward them, as if they were possible to miss. "It's been over twenty-four hours since their last feeding. Once our champions enter the arena, it's not only each other they'll be fighting!"

The crowd burst into cheers again.

The other champions and I were sitting in the Royal Box. Behind us, Empress Sorcha and Julian sat on their thrones. But I didn't need her soothing touch to control the lightning sparking under my skin. I could control it myself. And I wasn't worried about this fight.

Felix was going to stand back and let Cillian destroy Octavia. And judging by the way Cillian had been stomping around the villa since Julian had announced who he was sending to the arena, he was ready to show the full extent of his power.

I couldn't wait to see it.

I glanced back at Julian, and he gave me a confident nod.

"And now!" Bacchus raised his scepter and purple magic beamed out of it, up to the hole in the curtain covering the top of the building. "Let the fight begin!"

His magic reversed an illusion spell up above, revealing Octavia, Felix, and Cillian trapped in individual nets of vines. Cillian was directly across from the Royal Box. Octavia and Felix were off to the other sides, so they were opposite one another.

The vines bound their bodies, from their necks

down to their toes. Their hands were chained behind them, stuck inside bulky metal gloves that went up to their elbows.

"The gloves the champions are wearing were forged by Vulcan!" Bacchus announced as he floated over to watch from a safe spot above the crowd, within the boundary the gods had created to protect the audience. The orbs remained in the protective boundary, too. "They block the champions' magic. Once they escape the vines, the gloves will unlock, and they'll be able to use their powers!"

The crowd continued to cheer, and thick ropes of vines lowered the champions from the ceiling. They stopped once they were dangling about fifteen feet above the animals prowling below.

The three of them were already struggling to escape the vines. Cillian fought and contorted the most, his face twisting in anger as the vines tightened around his bulging muscles. He grunted and tried to push his way out of them, and they squeezed more.

Octavia struggled as well. Like Cillian, the vines around her tightened the more she fought.

Felix didn't fight the trap at all. He was following through on his promise. He wasn't going to escape, so Cillian and Octavia could face off one-on-one.

But unlike Cillian and Octavia's traps, the vines around Felix relaxed. The ones around his neck unraveled completely. The ones directly below it did the same.

His face flashed in panic, and he thrashed about, trying to reach for the vines above him to hold onto them. At his sudden movement, the vines tightened, trapping him again. The ones that had already released him hung limply where they were, but the others fought back as he squirmed.

Cillian's face was bright red. He was too caught up in trying and failing to break out of his trap using brute force to notice Felix.

Octavia wasn't.

She closed her eyes and went completely still, like she was in a meditative state. It didn't even look like she was breathing.

The vines unraveled one by one, starting with the ones around her neck and ankles.

Cillian was fighting so hard that his trap had twisted around, so his back was toward Octavia.

The gods knew he had a temper. They'd designed this competition against him.

My muscles tensed. Cillian needed to get ahold of himself so he could get free and take down Octavia. Instead, he screamed, so full of unbridled rage that one would have thought he could have ripped free of the vines with brute force if they didn't keep getting tighter the harder he fought.

He was going to be choked unconscious if he kept this up.

Maybe that'll be good. If he's unconscious, the vines will let him go.

But then the wild animals would pounce. So no, going unconscious definitely wouldn't be good for him.

Felix continued to squirm just enough to ensure the vines remained wrapped around him. He glanced back and forth between Cillian and Octavia, clearly realizing what was going on.

Tell Cillian to stop fighting! I thought. *Tell him, so he can face off against Octavia!*

I'd yell it myself if they'd be able to hear me. But the magic surrounding the arena prevented the champions from hearing anything that would affect the fight. Felix was the only one who could help Cillian.

But he said nothing.

It didn't take long for the last vine to unwrap around Octavia. She landed perfectly on her feet, and her gloves unlocked, clattering to the ground.

She flexed her fists, her blue magic swirling around her hands and up her arms. The first of the wild animals

—a lioness—pounced at her. But she held out her hands and flung an icicle straight into the lioness's heart when it was midair. She stepped to the side, and the lioness crashed to the ground next to her, dead.

She fought animal after animal, warding them off two at once. Cillian—who'd missed seeing how she'd escaped—fought the vines harder and harder as he watched her take one animal out after the other. The vines dug deep into his skin, and his blood dripped onto the ground beneath him.

The scent distracted the remaining animals. Enough of them ran toward the puddle of blood that Octavia had time to hop onto one of the hilly mounds. Her magic swirled around her body, and she thrust it out, creating a wall of ice that circled her completely.

A tiger ran at the wall, and bounced backward. The ice didn't even crack.

"Stay up there!" she yelled to Felix, who was still struggling the perfect amount to remain tied up by the vines without suffocating himself. "I've got this."

He did as she asked. Which I couldn't blame him for, since the gods hadn't provided them with any weapons, and his magic couldn't protect him from the beasts.

But why wasn't he helping Cillian?

The answer slammed into me, and anger boiled in

my blood. Felix had betrayed us. He was working with Octavia.

I never should have trusted that lying, arrogant jerk.

No longer having to worry about warding off the animals, Octavia faced Cillian, who was still struggling and bleeding in his trap. He thrashed harder as he tried to break free. His entire body was red from anger—and from being strangled.

She flung an icicle as long as a sword straight at him.

He was moving so much that it missed his heart and grazed his arm. It hit the magical boundary behind him that protected the crowd and shattered.

Octavia cursed and threw another icicle at him. It pierced his leg. The next was inches short from his head.

The fourth went straight through his heart.

Cillian went limp in the trap. The vines loosened and dropped him to the ground, his dead, mangled body landing in a heap on top of his spilled blood.

The animals leaped, ready to feast. But Bacchus's purple magic struck them down, and they disappeared into piles of ashes. At the same time, Felix's vines released him and dropped him to the ground, where he landed perfectly on his feet.

He refused to look at any of us sitting in the Royal Box.

Octavia hurried toward him, her face filled with worry as she examined him to make sure he was okay. As if it even mattered. Vejovis would heal any injuries they'd sustained in the fight.

A disgusted pit swirled in my stomach as I watched the concerned way Octavia touched Felix. He pulled her closer, cupping her face in his hands as he assured her he was all right and told her how amazing she'd been out there.

Hadn't he been telling us how much he hated touching her only a few nights ago?

I glanced at Cassia. It was clear from the tears that she was brushing away that she felt a million times more betrayed than I did.

Bacchus drove his chariot in a celebratory circle and landed next to Cillian's body. "Cillian—the chosen champion of Pluto—is officially out of the Games!" he said. "His soul is on its way to Elysium, where he'll be honored as a god for all eternity. May his crossing to the Underworld be a peaceful one!"

"May his crossing to the Underworld be a peaceful one!" the crowd repeated in unison.

I sat there, empty, as I listened to their creepy chant. The Games had beaten me again.

But I was done sitting on the sidelines.

Octavia might have survived this week. But the Games were far from over.

Next week, I wanted her in the arena again.

And I intended to be in there with her, so I could take fate in my hands and knock her out of the Games once and for all.

11

SELENA

"WE NEVER SHOULD HAVE TRUSTED FELIX," I said, snuggling into Julian's arms after an emotionally charged repeat of the other night.

It was his final night in the suite. Tomorrow, the room would belong to whoever won the next Emperor of the Villa competition.

"Agreed." He ran his fingers tenderly along my arm. "This should prove as a reminder that in the Games, we can only trust each other."

"We can also trust Cassia," I reminded him. "She's my best friend in the Games."

"I know she is." He reached for my hand and squeezed it. "And I believe her allegiance to us is real. But we always have to be on the lookout. Even around the ones we trust."

"Even when I'm around you?" I teased.

"Never." His eyes burned with so much intensity that I nearly stopped breathing. "We're soulmates. If I hurt you, it hurts me tenfold. I learned that the hard way when we met. I never want to do that to you again."

I nodded, since I knew what he meant. The time before realizing Julian was my soulmate had been agonizing. At least now I understood why I felt the way I did.

I was falling in love with him. I'd *been* falling in love with him since the moment I'd first seen him.

It was such a relief to no longer need to resist it.

He tilted his head curiously. "What are you thinking about?" he asked.

I bit my lower lip, hesitant to share. Because yes, we were soulmates. But was love something that happened at first sight? Or did it grow to exist over time? I craved Julian's touch, and I felt safe around him. But was that love? Or was it lust growing into love?

Was my confusion about this the reason why I wasn't ready to give myself to him completely?

Before I could put my thoughts into words, someone knocked on the door.

We hurried to make ourselves presentable, and then Julian walked over to look through the peephole.

He threw the door open, scowling. "Felix," he said,

blocking the entrance so Felix couldn't come in. "That was quite the show you put on in the arena."

"You're angry," Felix said.

"You think?"

They stared at each other, neither one of them backing down. I clenched the comforter, reining in the urge to shoot a lightning bolt at Felix's arrogant face.

"I can explain." Felix stood taller to look over Julian's shoulders. "Want to let me in?"

"No," Julian said. "But I will. Just so you can amuse us with whatever lie you think we'd be foolish enough to believe."

He stepped aside, and Felix strolled into the room, situating himself on the couch as comfortably as Venus had done when she'd stopped by a few days ago.

Julian slammed the door shut and sat at the foot of the bed. I joined him. It was two against one, and I was happy to make that clear.

"You're working with Octavia." I jumped straight to it. "You wanted her to win that competition."

"You're wrong," he said. "I'm with our alliance of four. I came up here to make sure you knew that."

"Our alliance is over," Julian said. "But please. Humor us."

"You have to understand," Felix started. "I didn't have a choice."

"We always have choices," I said. "And today, you made the wrong one."

"Will you please let me finish?"

Electricity crackled through me. But I took a deep breath and nodded, since the sooner Felix was out with it, the sooner he'd leave.

"Thank you." He gave me a knowing smile that only made me angrier. "I swear I'm not with Octavia. But if I'd openly helped Cillian, Octavia's entire side of the house would come after me. Possibly *including* Octavia, if Cillian didn't beat her."

"So you were saving your own skin," I said flatly.

"Of course," he said. "Can you blame me for wanting to stay alive?"

I said nothing, since no, I didn't blame him for that. But it didn't mean his point was valid.

"Cillian was strong," Julian said. "If you'd told him how to escape the vines, he would have defeated Octavia. That was why I put you in there with them. So you'd let him do the dirty work for us."

"It was never part of our deal that I'd openly help Cillian or go against Octavia," Felix said. "I was supposed to sit back, do nothing, and let them duke it out. That's *exactly* what I did by staying trapped in those vines."

"You stayed trapped because you wouldn't have survived against those animals," I said.

"That's true, and I'm confident enough about my myriad of other skills to admit it," he said. "But again, I never went against our deal. I'm just as sorry that Octavia beat Cillian as the two of you are."

"I highly doubt that," I muttered.

"But you know I'm right," he said smugly.

"I know what I saw out there," I said. "You care about Octavia. You wanted her to win."

"You think I *enjoy* touching her?" he snarled. "You think I'm looking forward to her coming to me tonight, wanting me to give myself to her again to celebrate her victory? You don't like her, but at least you don't have to pretend you do. At least using your powers against her doesn't mean letting her use your body in any way that pleases her."

His voice dripped with so much disgust that I nearly believed him.

"The two of you should be grateful for my loyalty," he continued. "I risked my life by going to the arena during your reign. I'm keeping this facade up with Octavia for the two of you—and for Cassia. All I want is to be with Cassia, and for everyone else in the house to know she's the only one I want. But I can't. Because then

Octavia and Antonia would come after her in a rage of jealousy, and I won't allow them to do that to her."

Julian scooted closer to me, although he kept his gaze on Felix. "You're sleeping with Antonia, too?" he asked.

"Not unless I have to." Felix's eyes were hard. "But this was what I signed up for when we made our alliance. It's what I was destined for when Venus chose me as her champion."

"We choose our own destinies," I said.

"We do," he agreed. "And I'm choosing to do whatever's necessary to keep the four of us alive for as long as possible. Don't turn on me because you don't like hearing about it. The fact is that Octavia still believes I'm on her side. We can use her trust in me to get her out of the Games."

"Because that worked so effectively today," I said.

"Did you not hear a word of what I just said?"

"I did," I said. "And I don't like it."

"Look." He ran his hand through his hair in frustration. "I'm not asking you to like me. I'm asking you to *work* with me. Your boyfriend sees my point here. Don't you, Julian?"

I turned to Julian, ready for him to back me up.

He wouldn't meet my eyes.

"Felix is right about our agreement," he said steadily.

"He promised to stand back and let Octavia and Cillian duke it out in the arena. That's exactly what he did."

"Seriously?" I couldn't believe it. "You're siding with him?"

"This isn't about sides," he said, and in that moment, it wasn't my soulmate beside me—it was the cold and lethal chosen champion of Mars. "It's about facts. The fact is that Felix never agreed to openly help Cillian. We both may have wanted him to, but his reasons for not doing so are valid."

"So what?" I said. "We're just going to forgive him and act like this never happened?"

Julian pressed his lips together, saying nothing.

This couldn't be happening.

"What about Cassia?" I turned back to Felix, rage coursing through my veins. "Do you really think she'll want anything to do with you after seeing you with Octavia today?"

"I don't just think it," he said. "I *know* it."

"Come on." I rolled my eyes. "I saw how betrayed she looked, watching you hold Octavia. There's no way she was faking that."

"It's hard for her," he said solemnly. "I wish it didn't have to be like this. But I spoke with her right afterward —while the two of you were up here canoodling."

"We weren't *canoodling*." I crossed my arms, hating Felix more and more with every word he spoke.

"Save it for someone who can't sense it," he said, and I bristled at the reminder of how intrusive his magic was. "The point is that I spoke with Cassia. She understands why I had to do what I did. She understands that it's all for her. She trusts me, and she trusts our alliance."

"I'll believe it when I hear it," I said. "From *her*."

"Deal accepted." Felix smirked.

"I didn't mean it like that."

"Then how did you mean it?" he challenged. "Because you have to see the logic in what I said. Or don't you? If that's the case, I'm happy to explain again."

"I understand what you said." I held up a hand, stopping him. "But that doesn't mean I like it."

"But you want to get far in the Games. And you know that means keeping me in the alliance, whether you like me or not."

I glared at him, hating that he was right.

Julian looked back and forth between Felix and me, as unemotional as ever. "This week didn't go as planned," he finally said, his commanding voice grabbing both of our attentions. "But if we continue working together, we need to come to an understanding. It's time to draw a line in the sand. Which means no more pawns from here on out. Until the final four, whenever any of us wins Emperor of the Villa, we won't put anyone in our group in jeopardy again. We're sending three strong players we *want* to get out of the Games to the arena. Maybe Octavia will lose against them, or maybe she won't. But at least we'll knock out her allies. Without them by her side, she'll crumble eventually. We'll make sure of it."

"I like the sound of that," Felix said.

Julian turned to me. "Selena?" His eyes begged me to say yes. To trust him.

I wanted to. But there was one other person in this villa that I trusted, too.

"Maybe," I said. "But first, I'm talking to Cassia."

"I already told you that I did that." Felix leaned back in the couch, his arms spread out as he let out a heaving, frustrated sigh.

"I'm sure you did," I said, since it was too big of a lie for him to make up without it biting him in the ass later. "But I need to hear it from her."

"And once she confirms it?"

"Then yes." It pained me to say it, but I needed to do what was best for me, Julian, and Cassia. And as unfortunate as it was, it meant honoring our deal with Felix. "If she's truly okay with what happened today, then I'll agree to those terms, and our alliance will continue."

TORRENCE

THE BOOKS TOLD us more about the objects King Devin had requested.

But they didn't mention where they could be found.

"Have any of you wondered *why* King Devin wants these objects?" Reed eventually asked.

"He wants to trade them for objects that'll get us to the Otherworld. You know this." I kept my eyes on the text in front of me, quickly returning to my research on Circe and her staff.

"That's not what I mean," he said. "It's just that these are all powerful objects. I'm curious about what he intends to do with them once he has them."

"King Devin will be handled," Thomas said confidently. "Whatever he wants with these objects, the other kingdoms and Avalon will keep him in check."

"We've had two prophetesses that we trust direct us to him," Sage added. "They wouldn't have done that if they knew another way to rescue Selena."

"All right, all right." Reed shrugged and pulled the book he was reading back onto his lap. "I was just wondering."

I glared at him out of the corner of my eye and continued my research. If he was trying to get us to question giving the objects to King Devin, he wasn't going to get anywhere.

After what felt like hours, someone came padding down the steps.

My mom.

"The four of you have been up all night," she said. "Haven't you?"

I glanced at my watch, surprised to see it was morning already. "I guess so."

"As thrilled as I am to see you showing an interest in the archives, it's time to put the books down and come back upstairs," she said. "Because you have a visitor."

Waiting on the white living room sectional, sipping a cup of tea, was a vampire I'd recognize anywhere.

Rosella.

I froze and stared at her. The legendary prophetess was casually drinking tea *in my living room.*

She wore Haven whites, although a bright, bohemian-style handbag rested at her feet. With her long dark hair and sightless cloudy eyes, she looked just like the illustrations from the picture books we read in lower school about the Earth Angel and the Queen of Swords.

"Thank you, Amber, for fetching them," Rosella said to my mom, her milky eyes staring straight at the wall in front of her. "Now, if you'll excuse us, I need an audience with the four of them alone."

"Of course." My mom bowed her head and hurried off to the kitchen, where she'd no doubt busy herself preparing a lavish breakfast—while trying to eavesdrop, of course.

"Torrence." Rosella looked in my general direction. "Cast a sound barrier spell, please."

I chuckled and did as requested.

She placed her teacup down on her saucer with extremely accurate precision given that she couldn't see. "Supernaturals have generally been blind to the fact that the ancient myths exist, because it was the will of the ancient creatures that it be so." She was apparently foregoing introductions and jumping straight to the point. "They wanted nothing to do with the quarrels and politics of the supernaturals on Earth. So naturally, they cast a spell to stop their paths from crossing ours. After enough time passed, they were no longer thought of as real, but as myth. However, now that you know they're real, you'll be able to find them and fight them."

"How do you know this?" Reed asked.

"I'm a prophetess," she said. "I know whatever I need to know to help whoever I need to help." She reached into her handbag and pulled out a thick, yellowing parchment. She unfolded it, laid it on the coffee table, and flattened out the creases. "The four of you need my guidance. So stop being shy, and come sit down."

We gathered around the coffee table. The parchment she'd spread out was a rudimentary map that reminded me of the ones pirates used to find treasure in television shows and movies.

It showed the exact locations of the objects King Devin had requested.

"This shouldn't be too hard," I said as I examined the map.

"Don't be fooled," Rosella said. "The challenge isn't *where* to find the objects. The challenge is *acquiring* them. And as I'm sure you've come to realize, only the four of you can go on this quest. If you bring anyone else along, you're destined to fail."

"Got it," Sage said, even though Rosella was right, and we'd already figured that out ourselves.

"Is there anything else we need to know that will help us?" Thomas asked.

"The fate of the world is at stake, and the four of you are an important piece of the puzzle to save it." She picked the map back up, folded it, and handed it to me. "But I came here to give you the map, and *only* to give you the map. Telling you any more may negatively impact the outcome of the mission. So I wish you a safe journey, and good luck."

13

SELENA

THE NEXT EMPEROR of the Villa competition didn't go as we'd hoped.

It was an arrow shooting competition.

Naturally, as the chosen champion of Apollo, Antonia won. The gods had clearly designed the competition in her favor.

But why?

That was what my alliance had gathered the next morning to discuss. Everyone tended to sleep in on Sunday morning, so the four of us woke early, headed to the bathhouse, and gathered in one of the most private areas in the villa apart from the emperor suite. The sauna.

Julian and I made extra effort to keep a friendly amount of space between us.

Cassia and Felix, on the other hand, sat so close that their legs touched. Her green wings always seemed to sparkle more when she was around him.

"Antonia's allegiances are unclear," Cassia said. "With her as Empress of the Villa, we're all at risk of being sent to the arena this week."

"That's why the gods wanted her to win," Julian said. "They love forcing players who are floating through the Games to pick a side."

Felix leaned back onto the wooden wall, not looking worried in the slightest.

Cassia mimicked his action, so now their shoulders touched along with their legs.

"We just have to convince Antonia not to send any of us to the arena this week," Felix said. "It shouldn't be hard."

"No." Anger flared through me, and I saw crackles of light in the corners of my eyes.

Julian jerked back in surprise. "Why not?" he asked.

"Because every week so far, Octavia has been victorious," I said. "Either in the arena, or in the Emperor of the Villa competition. The only way to make sure she's the one being targeted in the arena is to do it with our own hands. So I want to go to the arena this week. And I want her to be in there with me."

I'd expected Julian to immediately say no.

But he studied me for a few seconds, saying nothing.

His silence unnerved me.

"Only if I'm in there with you," he finally said. "Octavia's powerful, but so are we. The odds are in our favor if she's forced to face off against both of us."

My heart raced with happiness, and it took all of my willpower not to close the space between us and snuggle into him, like Cassia was doing with Felix. Because Julian's acceptance of what I wanted meant he believed in me, he believed in my magic, and he believed I was capable of facing off against Octavia.

Cassia looked back and forth between the two of us like we'd lost our minds. "Are you both serious?" she finally asked. "I thought we'd agreed that none of us would be pawns again."

"We agreed that if any of us won Emperor of the Villa, we wouldn't send any of the three others in our alliance to the arena," I said. "This doesn't go against that deal."

"It actually keeps us in control of the Games," Julian said. "It's a solid strategy."

"Care to explain?" Cassia asked.

"Octavia's not only powerful, but she's smart," Julian said. "If Antonia sends her to the arena with two other players who aren't in alliance, I'd bet that Octavia would team up with one of them to take the other out. Like she did with Emmet to take out Molly."

"And the longer she remains in the Games, the more likely she'll be to come after me and Julian, again and again," I continued. "We need to take her out now. But we can't trust anyone except ourselves. So the only way to ensure she's put on the defense is to ensure she's facing off against two physically strong players in *our* alliance."

"And I'm guessing you don't want to volunteer." Julian looked to Cassia.

Cassia lowered her gaze, not meeting either of ours.

"It's okay," I assured her. "Octavia has it out for me and Julian—not for you. It makes sense for the two of us to go in there against her."

"As long as you're okay with it…"

"Of course I'm okay with it," I said. "I volunteered."

"With the two of us in there together, we can't lose." Julian's eyes shined with belief in me—no, with belief in *us*.

"I want to say that the two of you are awfully full of yourselves, but I see your point," Felix said, looking to Julian. "Whenever you've been in danger around Selena, her magic explodes. First there was that fight against Cerberus that you told me about. Then that lightning bolt she called down from the sky to stop Bridget from stabbing you…" He paused and looked at me. "That was impressive."

"I didn't mean to do it." My stomach twisted as the image of Bridget being electrocuted to death flashed through my mind again. "It just happened."

"It happened because Bridget put Julian in danger," Felix said. "The two of you have it bad for each other. You're trying to hide it, but you don't have to around us. Because your relationship makes you stronger. And therefore, it makes our alliance stronger. What's there not to like about that?" He crossed his arms triumphantly.

"Are you both sure about this?" Cassia asked. "Absolutely, one hundred percent sure?"

"Yes," I said, and Julian said the same.

"Perfect." Felix sat straight and rubbed his hands together. "I'll work my magic on Antonia tonight. Make sure she does what we want."

Cassia's eyes narrowed into jealous slits, and she sat up, too, moving slightly away from Felix. "How, exactly, are you going to do that?" she asked.

"I'll do whatever it takes. Even if it means putting myself at her mercy. That's my part in this alliance. You know that." He took both of her hands and gazed lovingly into her eyes. "But you're the only one I want to be with."

"I know." She bit her lower lip, and I shifted uncomfortably. "I just wish it didn't have to be this way."

"Me, too," he said. "But I'm with *you*—not with any of them. Remember that. Always."

She rested her forehead against his and closed her eyes, breathing deeply like she was taking in every piece of him.

I stood up, and Julian did the same. "I think we've covered everything," I said, my cheeks flushing just from watching Cassia with Felix. Over the past few weeks she'd come to feel like a sister to me, and seeing her like that with him felt off. "We'll give the two of you some privacy."

I looked over to Julian, but he was already at the door.

He opened it and revealed Octavia standing on the other side, her hands clenched to her sides as she glared at us like a goddess out for revenge.

14

SELENA

CRAP.

"How long have you been out here?" I asked Octavia, glancing at Felix and Cassia.

Felix had already stood up, stone-faced as he looked at Octavia.

Cassia was hunched over on the bench, focusing on her feet.

"Long enough." Octavia scowled at Felix. "I was worried when it was taking you so long to come back to bed. Now I see you were busy leading on that *whore*."

Cassia's head snapped up. Her green magic floated out of her palms, swirling around her in a shield of protection.

"Cassia," I warned, since it was against the rules to

physically harm each other when we weren't playing in an official competition.

She swallowed and reined her magic in.

Octavia marched forward to stand right in front of where Cassia was sitting. "You really think he wants to be with someone as plain as you, when he has *me*?" she asked, each word dripping with hate.

I moved to Cassia as fast as lightning, sitting down and putting my arm around her shoulders. "Cassia's a better person than you could ever be." Electricity hummed under my skin as I glared up at Octavia. "Everyone in this house hates you. Felix included."

It slipped out before I realized it would blow our cover. Even so, I didn't want to take it back.

"Shut up, Princess. I wasn't talking to you. I was talking to *her*." She refocused on Cassia. "You're sleeping with him, aren't you?"

Cassia opened her mouth, like she was about to deny it. Then she closed it.

Oh my God. Is Octavia right?

I knew Cassia and Felix cared about each other. But she'd never been with a man before. She only wanted to be that intimate with her one true love. She'd told me that during the first few days of the Games.

If she'd given herself to Felix, surely she would have told me?

Like how you've been so open with her about Julian being your soulmate?

"You're worse than a whore." Octavia smirked down at Cassia. "You're his second choice. How does it feel, knowing that he's having you in the shadows while *I'm* the one he brings to his bed?"

"Enough." Felix put himself between Cassia and Octavia and stared Octavia down. "There's nothing going on between me and Cassia. You know me better than that."

Cassia stiffened, and I held onto her tighter.

"I know what I heard." Octavia backed away toward the door, each word low and measured. "So apparently, I don't know you at all."

She spun and ran out of the sauna before he could reply.

Cassia burst into tears in my arms.

Felix kneeled down in front of her and took her hands in his. But she pulled them away.

"Is she right?" Cassia sounded so vulnerable, and even though I wanted to trust everyone in our alliance, I was wondering the same thing.

"Of course not." Felix's eyes glistened with tears. "*You're* the one I love. I've told you that from the start."

I sat up, startled by the word *love*. I knew he and

Cassia cared for each other—at least, I knew Cassia cared for him. But *love*?

That was more than Julian and I had said to each other, and we were soulmates.

At the thought, I looked to Julian. He was standing next to the door, looking like he desperately wanted to leave Felix and Cassia to sort this out on their own.

He could do whatever he wanted. I wasn't leaving Cassia unless she asked me to.

"But what you just said…" Cassia's voice shook, and she couldn't continue.

Felix reached for her hands again. This time, she didn't pull away. "Yes, I've been with Octavia," he said. "I'm doing what I have to do to protect you. I've been open with you about that from the beginning, because I respect you. That's more than I could ever say about Octavia. She means nothing to me."

"How do I know you're not saying the same things to her that you're saying to me?" she asked.

"Because I didn't go after her just now. I stayed here with you. Surely that shows you that you're the one I love?"

Cassia sniffed and removed one of her hands from his to wipe away her tears. "What about tonight?" she asked. "When you go up to Antonia's suite to convince her to go along with our plan?"

"I'll do whatever it takes to get her on board." His face softened, making him look as vulnerable as ever as he remained kneeled at her feet. "Especially because now, you're on Octavia's radar. We *have* to get her out this week. To keep you safe."

But this was the Faerie Games. None of us were safe. It was just a question of who went sooner, and who went later.

From the heavy silence in the room, I had a feeling that the three of them were all thinking the same thing.

"If neither of us wins the Games, we'll be together in Elysium." Felix held tighter onto Cassia, begging her to believe him. "*Forever.*"

Cassia trembled, like she was about to burst into tears again. But she managed to get ahold of herself. "Selena?" she said, shifting to look at me. "Would you and Julian mind letting Felix and me continue this conversation in private?"

Yes, I do mind, I wanted to say. Because everything Felix was saying didn't sit right with me.

But Cassia could make her own decisions. This was what she wanted, and I needed to respect that.

"Of course." I let go of her and stood up. "But I'll have to make sure to stay away from Octavia, to stop myself from zapping the hell out of her."

That got a small chuckle out of Cassia, and then I

headed toward Julian, leaving with him so Felix and Cassia could be alone.

15

TORRENCE

MY MOM DROVE us to the airport, where Sage had called on the Montgomery jet to fly us directly to Nassau, Bahamas. All of the mythological objects were on the various uninhabited—well, *seemingly* uninhabited—Bahamian Islands.

Neither Reed nor I had ever been to the Bahamas, so we couldn't teleport the four of us there. And it was too big of a risk to study maps and pictures to try getting close. We could get stranded in the ocean. So, regular travel it was. And it was a good thing we were flying private, because getting through human airport security wouldn't have been easy, given all the potions and weapons we brought along with us.

The flight was at night, so we slept on the jet. We

landed at the Nassau airport at dawn, where a car was waiting to take us to a boat rental facility.

Thomas chartered one of the biggest yachts there. It came with a crew, but with Thomas's power over electronics, we didn't need them. The owner was hesitant to let us take the yacht without a crew, but a little compulsion from Thomas was all he needed to agree.

We stood on the top deck when we took off. I rested my arms on the railing, taking a deep breath of the salty ocean air. We were venturing into uncharted territory, and while I was excited, I was also scared of what might happen if we failed.

We won't fail, I told myself. *We'll get King Devin his objects, bring Selena back home, and everything will be back to normal.*

The pressure of saving my best friend's life was a never-ending weight on my shoulders. But all I could do was focus on one step at a time. Which meant following the map to get the first object.

We could do this.

Thomas stopped the yacht once we were far enough from Nassau that the island was a dot in the distance. "Torrence and Reed," he said. "It's time to create that boundary spell."

Witches couldn't place boundary spells around moving objects. But Reed had sworn that as a mage, he was powerful enough to do it—especially with the support of my magic. I hoped he was right. Because once we started collecting the objects, the only place to store them would be on the yacht. We needed a boundary spell to stop anyone—or any*thing*—from entering and trying to steal them.

We went downstairs and stood in the middle of the modern living room. Boundary spells extended outward, so it was best to cast them in the direct center of the place you were protecting.

"Take my hands," Reed said, handing his out to me.

I did as he said. His hands were surprisingly soft, warm, and comforting. And the way he was looking down at me with those dark, mysterious eyes…

Stop, I told myself. *You can't think about him like that. He's an ass. And he has a girlfriend back in Mystica.*

"Torrence?" he said, snapping me out of my thoughts.

"Yeah?"

"You ready to start?"

"Yep," I said, as casual as ever. "Let's do this."

Together, we chanted in Latin to cast the boundary spell. His yellow magic and my purple magic flowed out of our respective hands, spiraling around each other's to form a sparkling sphere around us. His eyes were locked on mine, trapping me in his intense—and encouraging —gaze.

We continued chanting, and my magic poured out of me faster than it ever had before. It swirled around us so quickly that my hair whipped across my face. Our magic was a tornado, and we were standing in the center of it.

My magic had always been strong. But I'd never created *wind* before.

Reed gripped my hands tighter and chanted louder. I did the same. His eyes glowed with his yellow magic, and while that never happened to witches, I was suddenly looking through a light purple lens, as if my eyes were doing the same.

He gave me a single nod, and I could feel what he was saying.

Do it now.

I nodded back in acknowledgment. Then we pushed out our magic, binding it to the yacht and creating a protective bubble around it.

The entire boat—plus the bubble around it—flashed yellow and purple, like an electric storm.

The final bits of magic released from our hands, and we stopped chanting. The colorful shield around the boat dimmed and turned nearly transparent. You'd only see the outline if you knew to look.

Wow.

My heart pounded as quickly as it did after finishing a great workout. I could somehow feel Reed's heartbeat through my hands, and it was synced with mine, beating just as fast.

I stood there, stunned, high from the incredible rush of power.

His eyes sparkled with a hint of his yellow magic, and I knew he felt it, too.

Whatever our magic had just done together... it wasn't normal. At least, I'd never heard of anything like it.

"Torrence?" he said my name slowly, like he was struggling to get ahold of himself.

I blinked, grounding myself in his steady gaze. "Did it work?" I asked.

"Thomas and I will get the boat going again to test it out," Sage said. She headed to the stairs that led up to the top deck, pausing at the bottom of them. "Come on, Thomas. You're the captain of this thing."

"I can connect to the boat's electrical system with my gift and tell it to move from here." He pressed his palm to the wall, and the engine revved to life.

"But we'll be able to see better from up there." Sage glanced at me and Reed, then looked back to her mate. "Come on."

Thomas opened his mouth to argue back. Then his lips formed a circle of understanding, and he followed Sage up to the deck.

My cheeks heated. They'd left me and Reed alone on purpose.

Awkward.

"You can let go of my hands now," Reed said. "Unless you're purposefully trying to cut off my circulation."

I glanced at where our hands were clasped together. Sure enough, I had his in a death grip.

"Sorry." I pulled away and rubbed my palms over my jeans. "That was…" I trailed off and gazed around the living room, still stunned by the incredible display of magic we'd just performed.

He stared at me, waiting for me to continue.

Focus, I told myself. *You sound like a bumbling idiot.*

"Did you feel it?" I asked.

"Feel what?"

"The magic…" I said. "The *power*. It was amazing. It was like our magic was feeding off each other's. Boosting it somehow."

He froze, expressionless. Then his eyes narrowed, and he looked at me like he was *disgusted* by me.

My breath caught in my throat. I stepped back and looked at the steps leading up to the top deck, ready to flee.

But then he spoke again, and his voice trapped me in place.

"Of course your magic felt boosted." He walked over

to the bar and poured himself a small glass of amber liquid. Hard alcohol of some sort. "I'm more powerful than you are. You were feeling *my* magic—not yours. That spell felt no different to me than any other." He took a sip of whatever he'd poured himself and puckered his lips. "Damn," he said, wiping his mouth with the back of his hand. "The humans who make this could learn a thing or two from the botanists in Mystica."

He placed the glass back down on the bar, clearly wanting nothing to do with it.

Anger rushed through me. Why did Reed always feel the need to "prove" that the mages did everything better than the supernaturals on Earth and Avalon?

"I know mage magic is stronger than witch magic." I straightened my shoulders, keeping my gaze level with his. "But that doesn't make you better than me."

"Did I say it did?" he asked.

No.

At least, not directly.

"Don't worry, little witch," he said. "It's okay for you to crave the rush of my power. I won't tell anyone." Then, he actually had the gall to *wink*.

"I don't *crave* your magic," I lied.

From his amused expression, I wasn't fooling either of us.

Ugh.

Fed up with his arrogance, I marched over to the bar, stared up at him in challenge, and picked up the glass of whatever he'd poured for himself. The liquid inside smelled like gasoline, but I took a sip anyway.

It took all my willpower not to cough and make a face. "I don't know what you're talking about. This is delicious," I said, forcing myself to take another sip. I was a bit more prepared that time. But still—yuck.

He raised an eyebrow. "You've had whiskey before?"

"Of course I've had whiskey before." I tossed my hair over my shoulder and leaned against the bar. "I don't live on Avalon full time, you know."

"Right," he said. "You spend your weekends on Earth."

"Yep." I took another sip, realizing how silly this all was. Forcing whiskey down my throat didn't prove I was as strong as Reed, or that I wouldn't be entranced by his magic if we needed to do another spell together in the future.

But I wasn't about to stand down now. So I took another sip, swallowing it down like it was as smooth as holy water.

He smirked, like he was waiting for me to show just a *hint* of dislike.

I didn't.

"Well, you enjoy that whiskey," he finally said. "I'm

going to check out the accommodations and get myself situated." He picked up his duffel and headed down to the rooms, not bothering to look back at me before going down the stairs.

I heard him open a door and shut it.

Once I was sure he was gone, I picked up the glass of whiskey, pinched my nose together to block out the foul stench, and poured it down the sink.

SELENA

Felix spent the night in Antonia's suite, exactly like he'd said he would.

Julian and I chatted with Cassia until she fell asleep, to take her mind off of it. It didn't work completely, but it was better than leaving her to her own thoughts.

The next morning, Felix and Antonia slept through breakfast. They emerged from her suite just in time for lunch. They both had dark circles under their eyes. But while Antonia was practically glowing despite her lack of sleep, Felix looked exhausted. It was the least perfect I'd seen him look during the entire time in the Games.

During lunch, Octavia made a big show of flirting with both Pierce *and* Emmet. But if she was trying to make Felix jealous, it wasn't working. His attention remained on Antonia.

Even though it was all for show, Cassia struggled to keep herself from looking at them through the entire meal. Each time she did, she looked like she'd been stabbed in the heart.

After eating, Cassia, Julian, and I retreated to the library.

"I know he has to give her attention until the selection ceremony is over," Cassia said once we closed the door behind us. "But that doesn't mean I have to watch it."

We continued to chat with Cassia about anything we could think of to keep her mind off of Felix and Antonia. She was a private person—she didn't talk much, if at all, about her life in the Otherworld. I suspected it made her sad to think about how she'd likely never return to her family. So she and Julian told me all about the history and stories of the Otherworld, while I told them about Avalon and Earth.

After about an hour, someone pushed the door open and came inside.

Felix. He rubbed his eyes and collapsed onto the sofa next to Cassia.

She scooted away from him. "Where's Antonia?" The jealously in her voice was impossible to miss.

"She went upstairs to take a nap," he said. "She asked

me to join her. I said I would, but that first, I wanted to work out."

As if he didn't get enough of a workout with her last night?

I would have said it out loud if Cassia weren't in the room. There was no need to make her feel worse than she already did.

"And the other three?" I glanced at the closed door.

"You saw Octavia." Felix smirked. "She's out there trying to make me jealous with Pierce and Emmet. As if I care." He moved closer to Cassia, directing that last part to her. She didn't move away again, although she remained expressionless. If he was trying to make her feel better, it didn't seem to be working. "Octavia has too much pride to come chasing after me."

"Agreed." Julian sat straighter and moved to the edge of his chair. "But we should discuss this quickly, just in case. How'd it go last night with Antonia?"

"Not exactly like we'd hoped." Felix sighed and ran his hand through his perfectly tousled hair.

My heart stopped. "What happened?" I asked.

"Antonia wants me to herself," he said. "She's jealous of all the other girls in the Games."

It would have sounded ridiculously arrogant coming from a normal guy who hadn't been gifted magic from Venus. Now, I realized he was simply stating a fact.

"She wants to make sure another girl is taken out of

the Games during her reign as Empress of the Villa," he continued. "And other than her, there are only three of you left…"

"Me, Octavia, and Cassia," I said flatly.

"Yep."

Cassia pulled her legs up onto the sofa and wrapped her arms around them. Her expression remained blank.

Felix tried to reach for her, but she shrugged him off.

He pressed his lips together and focused on Julian. "In Antonia's mind, Octavia's the biggest threat to my affections," he said. "So Octavia's her target. I tried my hardest to convince her that you and Selena would definitely team up, and that the two of you together had the best chance of successfully taking out Octavia."

"And?" I leaned forward, hoping he'd gotten Antonia to at least *consider* it. If he had, he still had time before the selection ceremony tomorrow to change her mind.

"She refused to listen. She wants to make sure it's one hundred percent going to be a girl going out this week. The only way to guarantee that is by sending three girls to the arena."

Felix's tone was final. And from Julian's steely gaze, he recognized the same thing I did. Felix's magic had worked *too* well on Antonia. She wasn't going to budge.

"This changes nothing," I said. "Cassia's a strong physical player, just like me and Julian. We fought well together against Emmet in the first Emperor of the Villa competition. We'll team up against Octavia, and we'll beat her. Just as planned."

"It changes *everything*." Cassia dropped her arms down to her sides. "We wanted you and Julian to fight together because his being in danger sets off your magic. Without Julian in there with you, that won't happen. Our chance of beating Octavia will be lowered."

"That's not true," I said, even though I *had* felt more confident about fighting with Julian than I did with Cassia. But we had the best chance of succeeding if she believed in herself as much as I believed in her. "Obviously none of you saw me fight the monsters on my path in the Emperor of the Villa competition this week. But I was on *fire*. I think that after Bridget…" I swallowed, unable to say the specifics of what I'd done to Bridget without crying. "What happened with her changed something in me. I controlled my magic and took down every monster in my path."

"You were the fifth to get to the center," Cassia pointed out. "And I didn't get to the center at all." A tear leaked out of the corner of her eye, and she wiped it away. "The harpy flew me right off the path."

"But you beat the first two monsters," Julian said. "Plus, the harpy dominates the air, and you dominate the earth. That challenge wasn't in your favor from the start."

"Maybe." She shrugged. "But I should have been able to do it. And I failed. Just like I would have failed fighting one-on-one against Emmet if Selena hadn't swooped in to help me."

"But the two of us together *did* beat Emmet." I leaned forward, gaining confidence with each word I spoke. "What happened before I teamed up with you is irrelevant. Because you won't be fighting one-on-one against Octavia. You'll be fighting with me. And we're going to win."

17

TORRENCE

"SCYLLA AND CHARYBDIS." I stood on the top deck of the boat, my hands on the railing as I stared out at the strait between cliffs ahead of us. I could just make out the six snake-like heads poking out behind the cragged rocks on the right. "I never thought I'd fight *Scylla and Charybdis.*"

"Just Scylla," Sage said. "We're staying far away from Charybdis. Well, as far away as possible." She shuddered when she said the whirlpool monster's name.

"Our plan is solid," Thomas said. "Kill Scylla, grab the girdle, and get out. It shouldn't be hard."

Easy for him to say. He'd fought monsters before.

This would be my first.

I hoped my training in Avalon was enough to prepare me.

"Scylla's only unbeatable for humans," Sage reminded me. "But against a mage, a witch, and two vampire/shifter dyads? She doesn't stand a chance."

"True," I said. "Thanks."

"I was scared before fighting my first monster, too." She gave me an encouraging smile. "But a little fear is a good thing. Overconfidence is your own worst enemy."

"Who knew you were so wise?" Thomas said.

Her smile widened. "And who knew you were such a comedian?"

Reed plodded up the steps before Thomas could reply, a black duffel bag thrown over his shoulder. "This is all of it," he said, dropping the duffel down in the middle of the deck.

Of course, he spoke only to Sage and Thomas. Not to me.

After the barrier spell incident, the four of us had gathered to discuss our strategy against Scylla. Reed didn't say a word to me the entire time. He didn't even *look* at me.

Whatever. I had more important things to worry about.

Like taking down Scylla.

Reed unzipped the duffel. Inside were three holy swords, one bow with a quiver full of arrows, and four vials of clear potion.

Thomas inspected the contents and nodded. "Now, we wait," he said.

We only had to wait an hour before the water on the left side of the strait opened up. The hole grew wider, the water around it swirling faster and faster.

Charybdis.

Nothing was in her path, so all she'd be getting was a meal of whatever unlucky fish were swimming by.

After about ten minutes, the angry, roaring whirlpool started to shrink, until the water was calm again.

Thomas checked his watch—a habit of his, since he could use his gift to know the time without having to look. "Looks like Charybdis had an early lunch," he said.

"You mean brunch?" Sage teased.

"Precisely," he said. "It'll be a few hours until her next meal. So, grab your weapons. It's time to strike."

Sage, Reed, and I reached for our swords. A large tanzanite gemstone was embedded above the handle of mine. Sage's had a ruby, and Reed's had a yellow quartz. There were holsters beneath them. We strapped them on our shoulders so the sheaths were at our backs, and slid our swords inside.

Thomas grabbed the bow and the quiver full of crystal tipped arrows. The crystal arrowheads were spelled so they'd always return to the quiver. That spell was courtesy of one of the former head witches of the Carpathian Kingdom who'd moved to Avalon a few years back.

Weapons in hand, we reached for our vials of potion. Sage uncapped hers first, and the rest of us followed.

Thomas raised his vial. "To taking down Scylla," he said.

"And to getting Aphrodite's girdle," I added.

We clinked our vials together, brought them to our lips, and downed the contents. The drink tickled my tongue, although it tasted like nothing—like air.

In seconds, the others faded until they were hazy ghosts with a white glow around them. I held my hand out in front of me. It looked like a hazy ghost, too.

That was the beauty of invisibility potion from the same batch. We could see each other, but no one could see us. At least for the hour that the potion remained in our systems. And because we were already holding our weapons, they'd gone invisible, too.

"Ready?" Thomas looked us over. "Okay."

I bit down a comment about him sounding like a character from my mom's favorite cheerleader movie.

Instead, I stepped back up to the front railing, breathing in the warm, salty air as we sailed toward the deadly strait.

18

TORRENCE

WE CAME around the cliff's jagged rocks, and the closest of Scylla's heads looked in our direction. It was just like the head of a snake, except these snakes were at least four times as long as the length of the yacht.

It opened its mouth, revealing three rows of crooked yellow teeth.

Then, it yelped. Like a small, yappy dog.

That set off the rest of them. Within a second, all six heads were looking our way and barking. The barks were amplified, but Scylla still sounded like a group of playful puppies.

It should have been impossible for giant snakes to make those sounds. Yet, here we were.

At least it made Scylla seem less scary. But only

slightly. Her massive body was attached to the cliff behind her, and her mouths were big enough to swallow even the biggest of humans whole. They chomped at the bit, salivating for their next meal.

We stopped right in front of Scylla. Her heads sniffed at the yacht, confused. Thanks to our cloaking rings, we weren't just invisible, but our scents were hidden, too.

Thomas strung an arrow through his bow, ready to strike. Once he did, that was our cue to attack.

The boat jolted, and he stumbled back.

I gripped the rail to steady myself.

A deep rumble behind us made the entire boat vibrate.

"It's Charybdis!" Reed yelled. "She's opening again!"

At the sound of his voice, one of Scylla's heads darted toward him. It crashed into the boundary surrounding the boat. Its eyes rolled around in a daze, like a cartoon character who'd run into a wall.

The head next to it tried the same thing. The boundary stopped it, too.

The other heads must have gotten the memo, because they stayed where they were, yapping louder at the yacht.

The boat creaked, and I spun to look behind us. The hole in the ocean had opened up again, and the water around it was starting to move in a circle. A flash of a tooth peeked out from under the surface.

Charybdis.

She was getting closer. Well, *we* were getting closer to *her*.

I looked to Thomas. His gift over electronics could control the boat's motor.

His brow was beaded in sweat.

Apparently, not even Thomas's gift could stop the boat from being pulled into the swirling current.

Reed ran to the other side of the deck, dropped his sword, and held both of his hands over the rail. Yellow magic poured out of them, straight toward the ocean below.

The boat jolted to a stop.

Charybdis's mouth was still widening, revealing a hideous circle of sharp teeth. But somehow, the yacht was no longer being pulled toward it.

It floated peacefully, like it was on a lake and not next to a deadly whirlpool.

"I need both of my hands to hold off the current," Reed said, not looking back at us. "The three of you need to take down Scylla on your own."

Great. Reed's mage magic was a major reason why fighting Scylla was supposed to be a breeze. And

Thomas needed to stay on the boat, to make sure it didn't float astray. His crystal arrows would hurt Scylla, but they wouldn't kill her.

The hard part was now on Sage and me.

"All right." Sage turned to me, her wolfish eyes flashing with excitement. "Ready to slice and dice?"

No.

"Ready as ever," I said instead, backing up in preparation to fight.

Sage did the same, and counted off. "One, two, three, GO!"

We ran across the deck. I kept my eyes on the snake I was heading toward—the one on the far right. I purposefully didn't look down before pushing off and jumping.

We were close to Scylla, so while I had to jump high, it was only a few feet forward. I'd practiced things like this so many times on the Avalon training courses that sticking the landing was a breeze.

I wrapped my legs around the neck, squeezing them to balance myself. The head thrashed around, trying to throw me off, but I dug my fingers into its scaly skin and held on.

Once I had a steady grip, I checked on Sage. She'd landed perfectly on the snake all the way to the left.

A glance at the dark water crashing against the boulders below showed me that I'd made the right decision by jumping before looking down.

With no time to waste, I removed my sword from the holster. The tanzanite gem glowed, and I swung the sword down on Scylla's neck. It sliced clean through.

Before the neck fell into the water, I hopped to my feet and jumped onto the snake next to me. Sage had done the same.

Two heads down, four to go.

The neck I was sitting on had a handful of holes in it already. Thomas's arrows. With the snake already weakened, it wasn't able to try as hard to knock me off.

He moved on to aim his arrows at the two heads in the center.

The yaps next to me grew louder.

I looked over my shoulder just in time to see the head to my right coming down on me, its mouth open like a cave ready to swallow me whole.

I raised my sword above my head, ready to ram it up through the roof of its mouth. But magic burst out of my palms and traveled up and out of the sword, spreading out in a shimmery purple boundary around me. Scylla's teeth chomped down, but on the boundary —not on me.

The head squeezed down with its teeth, trying to

break past the dome surrounding me. But I pushed out more magic to strengthen the shield. The dome expanded up and out to the sides. I heard the crack of bones breaking—the monster's jaw.

Buzzing from the high of the magic, I pushed out *more*.

The dome grew larger, and Scylla's head exploded from the inside out.

The neck fell, hitting the boundary around the yacht and sliding down into the ocean. The purple magic around me faded into nothing.

The neck I was sitting on bucked, but my legs were tight enough around it that I stayed on. The magic I'd used must have been keeping it still before.

Sword still raised, I sliced it through the neck, hopped onto my feet, and jumped back onto the top deck of the yacht. I landed just as the neck crashed into the boundary surrounding the boat.

Sage killed her final head and jumped back on deck. Scylla's final neck dropped into the ocean. Her body fell with it, making a loud sucking noise as it detached from the cliff and splashed into the water below.

It floated away from the yacht and was pulled into Charybdis's swirling vortex.

Sage, Thomas, and I ran to the other side of the deck just in time to see Charybdis swallow Scylla down. Her teeth closed around the end of Scylla's body, and the whirlpool slowed, coming to a stop. The ocean was calm once more.

Reed let go of his magic, turned so his back was on the railing, and slid to the ground.

"You okay?" Thomas asked.

"Yeah," he said, holding his head up with his hands. "That took a lot of magic. Give me a few minutes and I'll be good."

"You guys," Sage said from the opposite side of the deck. "Look."

I spun around and saw the cave entrance that had previously been hidden by Scylla's body. The cave was high up—a longer and higher jump than it had been to get to Scylla's necks, since the necks had slithered down to sniff us out.

"You stay here to keep the boat in place," Sage said to Thomas. "I've got this."

Sage dropped her sword and shifted into wolf form. She jumped onto the vertical cliff, digging into the slippery rocks with her claws to hold on. She easily scaled it up to the cave.

The three of us were silent as we waited for her to come out. Hopefully she was okay. Thomas was the only other one of us who could shift into a wolf and scale the cliff, but he was also the only one of us who could control the yacht. We needed him down here.

After a few tense minutes, Sage emerged from the cave. She was back in human form, and she was holding a woven, gold belt.

Aphrodite's magic girdle.

19

TORRENCE

"CATCH!" Sage said, and she tossed the girdle down to the deck.

I hurried over to where it was heading and caught it perfectly. It was a good thing that the boundary Reed and I had created knew what we wanted to keep out, and what we wanted to let in.

The girdle was heavier than I'd expected. And it was buzzing with magic.

Suddenly, Reed strode over to me, cupped my face with one of his hands, and gazed down at me with complete adoration. Then, he kissed me.

My heart jumped, and I sank into his embrace. Kissing him back was as natural as breathing, and I didn't want to ever stop.

But this wasn't like him.

Somehow, I forced myself to pull away.

His cheeks were flushed, and I was sure mine looked the same.

"What are you doing?" My voice was barely louder than a whisper. "You hate me."

"I don't hate you." He pushed some of my hair behind my ear, looking at me like I was the most precious thing to him in the entire world. "You're beautiful. I love you."

"You barely know me," I said. "You don't love me…"

Wait.

I glanced at the girdle in my hand. Then, I dropped it to the floor.

Reed blinked and stepped back. His dark eyes narrowed, and he wiped his lips with the back of his hand.

I needed to say something—anything—before he said something mean and spiteful.

"Looks like the girdle works." I forced myself to chuckle, even though my head was still spinning from Reed's kiss.

He stared at me, his hard expression giving no hint of any emotion. Not even hate or disgust. Just… nothing.

"No need to apologize," I continued, my tone as light as possible. "I know that was the girdle speaking—not you."

Reed frowned and turned to Thomas and Sage. Sage must have scaled back down the cliff and joined us sometime while Reed was kissing me.

"Let's get out of here before Charybdis opens her mouth again," Reed said. "Then we'll regroup and make a plan of attack for getting the next object."

He hurried to the stairs as Thomas started up the boat, glancing over at me on his way. I could have sworn his eyes flashed with the same longing they'd had in them right after he'd kissed me. But he disappeared below deck before I could tell for sure.

I stared at the place where he'd been, and my fingers drifted to my lips. They still tingled at the memory of how warm his had been on mine.

That kiss...

I replayed it in my mind, unable to forget how *right* it felt to kiss Reed.

I wanted to kiss him again. I wanted him to look at me like that again.

The girdle made him do it, I reminded myself, looking down at the cursed object at my feet. *None of that was real.*

Reed hadn't actually wanted to kiss me. Just like he hadn't meant it when he'd said he loved me.

"Well." Thomas shifted his feet and cleared his throat. "That was interesting."

"Did anything happen to you while I was holding the girdle?" I asked him.

"No," he said. "But nothing—not even that girdle—can overpower the mate bond." He looked over at Sage, and she moved closer to him to take his hand.

They smiled at each other, their eyes so lovey-dovey that it made me sick.

Why can't I have that?

I shook the thought away. Going down that road would bring nothing but heartache.

"You were awesome back there," Sage said, looking back at the strait. "Making Scylla's head explode? That was some kickass magic."

"It wasn't mine," I said.

"What do you mean?"

"I didn't chant a spell to create that boundary. It wasn't witch magic. It was…" I bit my lip, unable to say it out loud. Because it was ridiculous.

Sage let go of Thomas's hand and came over to lean on the rail next to me. "It was what?" she asked.

"It was mage magic."

"Hm." She tilted her head, studying me. "Is that possible?"

"I don't know." I shrugged. "When Reed and I created the boundary spell around the yacht, my magic connected with his. It felt stronger than ever. Maybe some of it was still left in me during that fight."

She took my hand, removed my cloaking ring, and sniffed. "You smell stronger than before," she said, putting the ring back on my finger. "That could explain why."

"So you think what? That Reed *gave* me some of his magic?" I laughed it off, since the thought was ridiculous.

"I have no idea," she said. "But it can't hurt to ask him."

"There's no point," I said. "He hates me. He'd never give me his magic."

"I don't think he *hates* you," she said.

"Um, yeah. He does."

"He's guarded," Thomas said as he finished wrapping the girdle inside of his jacket to keep it from direct skin contact. "Don't mistake that for hate. I was guarded once, too." He glanced at Sage, and his eyes softened, like they always did when he looked at her.

It was similar to how Reed had looked at me when I'd been holding the girdle.

Ugh.

"It was probably a remnant from the spell we did together," I decided. "It'll go away."

"Ooookay." From the way Sage elongated the word, I could tell she didn't believe it.

"How much farther until our next stop?" I asked Thomas, eager to change the subject.

"Not far," he said. "We need to head downstairs to strategize. Maybe pop a bottle of champagne while we're at it. After all, we did just get Charybdis to *eat* Scylla."

"That was pretty awesome, wasn't it?" Sage smiled.

"It was more than awesome," he said. "Because if knowledge serves me right, we made history with that one."

I followed them down the steps, reminding myself to forget about Reed and focus on the present. Because at the end of the day, the way Reed felt about me didn't matter.

All that mattered was getting the three remaining objects, giving them to King Devin, and saving Selena.

20

SELENA

CASSIA, Felix and I sat on the same sofa for Antonia's selection ceremony, with Cassia in the center.

Julian was in the armchair closest to me.

One plain golden orb remained floating in front of Antonia. The other two floated above her head, with holograms of Octavia and Cassia's faces in their centers.

Cassia and I had been holding hands from the start of the ceremony. She'd taken her selection so gracefully that she hadn't even stirred when her name was called. Octavia—who was sitting across from us—had done the same.

Antonia reached for the final orb. She hadn't bothered explaining why she'd chosen Octavia and Cassia, and I expected that this time would be no different.

"The final champion I'm sending to the arena is..."

She looked around at all of us, her eyes full of glee as she drew out what I knew was going to be the announcement of my name.

My grip on Cassia's hand tightened.

After a few unbearably long seconds, Antonia tossed the orb into the air.

Everything moved in slow motion.

I'm ready for this, I thought. *I can do this.*

The orb leveled out with the others above her head, and a face appeared in the center.

It wasn't mine.

No. I stared at the face in the orb, as if staring at it for long enough could make it change.

I should have felt relieved that I was safe this week. But my breathing shallowed, sparks flaring up inside of me as betrayal rattled me to the core.

Cassia's hand went limp in mine.

"Pierce, the chosen champion of Vulcan." Antonia smiled at him, and he beamed back. "You're the third champion I'm sending to the arena."

"Finally." He rubbed his hands together, and smoke drifted up from his palms. "Thanks, Antonia, for giving me a chance to show them what I'm made of."

"Anytime." From the way they were looking at each other, it was obvious that they'd planned this.

Electricity rushed through me. I pulled my hand out

of Cassia's, not wanting to shock her. The light glowed in spidery lines up to my elbows. Everyone in the room looked my way, and one of the many orbs zoomed to float above me.

"Selena?" Vesta asked. "Is there anything you want to say before the ceremony ends?"

I looked to Antonia. "You lied." I spoke steadily and slowly, focusing on reining in my anger.

"It's the Faerie Games," Antonia said with a conniving smile. "Everyone lies."

Her words punched me in the gut. Because they were true.

The only people I could trust in the Games were Julian and Cassia. I'd known that. Yet, I'd believed that Felix could control Antonia. *He'd* believed he could control Antonia.

Either he'd failed, or he was playing us. For Cassia's sake, I hoped it was the former. But I had a sinking feeling that it was the latter.

If—*when*—Cassia made it out of the arena this week, she, Julian, and I needed to win every Emperor of the Villa competition from next week forward. It was the only way to ensure our safety. We had the strength to do it, and we *would* do it.

I was raised by the leaders of Avalon, born of a powerful witch and a faerie prince, and gifted with magic from Jupiter. I wasn't going to let fear control me any longer.

It was time to show them what I was made of. And if the Nephilim army didn't come before Julian, Cassia, and I were the only ones remaining, I'd refuse to fight my soulmate and my closest friend in the Otherworld. I'd go against the gods before it came to that.

Decision made, my electricity dulled down to a low hum until it was no longer visible on my skin.

"Does anyone else have anything they wish to say?" Vesta asked.

No one said a word.

"Then this Selection Ceremony has come to a close."

21

SELENA

OCTAVIA, Pierce, and Emmet followed Antonia up to her suite after the ceremony.

Cassia buried her face in her hands and ran out of the library.

Felix and I stood up to go after her. But I zoomed to stand in front of him, blocking his path.

Surprise crossed his face, quickly followed by annoyance. "What are you doing?" he asked.

"Stopping you."

"May I ask why?"

"Because bombarding her isn't going to help her," I said. "She needs time with someone she can trust."

"Which is why I'm going to her." He looked down at me and narrowed his eyes, like he was trying to put me in my place.

But I hadn't been intimidated by him before, and that wasn't going to change now.

"You have no idea how much it hurt her to see you parading around with Antonia these past two days," I said. "But I was there. I saw it all. And I was the one who was there for her. Not you."

"It hurt me, too." His eyes were so cold that goose-bumps rose on my skin. Was he trying to conceal his pain? Or did he just not feel anything at all? "But I did what I did to help her. She knows that."

"You failed her." I didn't bother hiding my contempt.

"I did my best," he said. "And it wasn't enough."

"You're right. It wasn't. And seeing you will only remind her about how much you let her down."

His face crumpled in pain.

Maybe he did actually care for her?

I didn't know. But now wasn't the time to figure it out.

"I'm going to her," I repeated. "If she tells me she wants to see you, I'll let you know."

I marched past him, expecting him to continue fighting over the issue.

But he stood there and let me go.

Cassia was curled up under the covers in her bed. Her wings poked out of the top, the green duller than normal. She peeked out from under the covers when she heard me come in. Her eyes were tear-stained and red.

I sat down on the bed next to hers—my bed—and leaned against the headboard. There was no point in asking her if she was okay. She clearly wasn't.

I searched for the perfect words, but none entered my head.

She wiped her eyes and sat up, mirroring my position. "They planned this," she said. "Antonia, Octavia, and Pierce planned this to get me out."

I wished I could say it wasn't true.

But we'd both know it would be a lie.

"Octavia must have told Antonia about me and Felix," she said.

"Maybe." I leaned on my side to face her. "But Octavia's one of the biggest threats in the Games. Pierce has every reason to want her out. We can talk to him. Get him to fight with you."

"He's working with them," she hissed. "You saw them go up with Antonia to her suite. Antonia, Octavia, Pierce, and Emmet." She counted them off on her fingers. "They're a team."

And maybe Felix, I thought, although of course I didn't say it out loud.

"We have three more days until the arena fight," I said instead. "We can swing Pierce over to our side."

"I hate this." She pulled her legs up to her chest and wrapped her arms around them. "I don't want to be here. I *never* wanted to be here."

"So why did you volunteer?" I asked.

Unlike me, most half-bloods volunteered to be nominated for the Games. They all had different reasons. Most wanted money, or magic, or an eternity of being honored as a god in Elysium.

Since half-bloods had no magic, the Faerie Games were pretty much their only way—except death—to escape a lifetime of servitude to the fae. Desperation could drive people to make incredibly crazy choices.

That was how I'd ended up here.

Desperation to get home, faith in the Nephilim army, and yeah, I *did* want magic of my own.

I was no different than the rest of them.

Cassia unwrapped her arms from around her legs and picked at the green polish on her nails. "My family lives a better life than most half-bloods," she finally said. "Me, my parents, and my two brothers."

This was the first time she'd ever mentioned her family. So I stayed quiet, waiting for her to continue.

"We have a large apartment close to the fae part of the city. Both of my parents are employed in a royal fae's household. We had ample food, and gave whatever we could spare to those less fortunate."

"That sounds lovely," I said, although I couldn't help noticing how she'd said they *had* ample food. Past tense.

"It is." She sniffed and gave me a half-smile. "Or at least, it was."

"What happened?" I spoke cautiously, wanting to learn about her life but also not wanting to pry.

"About a year ago, my father started going to the gambling hall." She lowered her eyes in shame. "At first it was only on the weekends. But then he started coming home from work later and later. We no longer had food to spare for those less fortunate. It didn't take long before things started disappearing from the house. Trinkets, silverware, the little jewelry my mom had—stuff he could sell. All we have left now is the furniture."

"So you volunteered for the Games to help your family."

"I didn't volunteer." Her eyes hardened. "My father thought I was sleeping the night when a fae came to our house, demanding he pay him back an enormous amount of coin that I knew we no longer had. I peeked out of my bedroom door, but the fae's back was toward me. All I saw were his sapphire wings.

"The next day at dinner, my father told us the truth. We had nothing left. Worse—we were in debt, so badly that not even ten years salary could pay it back. He said he kept thinking that if he just played a few more games —if he bet coin he no longer had—he could win it all back. Instead, he dug a hole so deep that we were going to lose our home."

"I'm sorry." I wished I could say something more to help her. But there was nothing more to say. And right now, she didn't need me to say anything.

She needed me to listen.

"But he said all wasn't lost," she continued. "He said there was a way out. And then, as if he were waiting for that exact moment, a fae came to our door, bearing sweets and honey wine. A fae with sapphire wings."

"The same fae from the night before."

"Yes." She swallowed, and then continued. "The fae joined us at our table and introduced himself as Prince Cormick. The son of the prince who employs my parents. He was the one who introduced my father to the gambling hall in the first place. But unlike my father, he was skilled in the games he played. The debt my father owed was mostly to him. And now, he'd come to collect.

"The entire time he spoke, his eyes were mostly on me." She glanced at the nearest orb, like she was speaking through it to the sapphire-winged prince himself. "Conniving, ambitious eyes that watched me like he owned me. I soon learned why. He and my father had come to an *arrangement*. The prince was going to nominate me for the Faerie Games, so my father could pay him back using the stipend my family would receive for my participation."

I swallowed down the disgust rising in my throat. "Over a hundred half-bloods were nominated for the Games." I needed to find some kind of flaw in her father's plan, even though it was already over and done with. "There was no guarantee you'd be chosen."

"My father's a gambling man." She chuckled, although it was far from funny. "He was willing to take the risk."

"You could have said no." I sat up, electricity crackling under my skin. "You *should* have said no."

Her eyes were wistful, like she was imagining a life where she'd done just that. "My older brother volunteered to go in my stead," she said. "But my father wouldn't risk the lives of his sons. And the fae was offering the opportunity only to me."

"So you said yes."

"I had to." She bit her lip, looking more vulnerable than ever. "They're my family."

I shook my head in disbelief. Cassia was kind—too kind, at times. Her father had used that to his advantage.

"Family doesn't gamble their daughter away like

she's worth no more than a pile of coins." My words were harsh, but true. And she didn't deny it.

"It's okay," she said, even though it wasn't. "I've found new family here. In you, and in Felix. I want one of you to win. I believe one of you *will* win. But if you don't, we'll always have Elysium."

"You're talking like you don't have a chance," I said.

"Because I don't." She shrugged.

"That's not true," I said. "You're powerful. You have to survive this week. I've told you all about my family—about Avalon, and the Nephilim army. They're coming for us—I know they are. We just need to stay alive long enough for them to get here."

Prince Devyn knew where I came from. He knew the strength of Avalon. The fae needed to know, too. Perhaps they'd even free me—or, better yet, end this year's Faerie Games—to avoid war against my realm.

"Your faith in the Nephilim is inspiring," Cassia said. "But the fae are a force to be reckoned with. Perhaps more so than your army."

Her words stabbed me in the heart. Because the longer I was here, the longer I was wondering if it might be true.

I had a plan if Julian and I were the only two left. But as hard as I tried to think it through, Cassia didn't fit into that plan. Which was why the Nephilim army *had* to make it here, and soon.

"We'll talk to Pierce," I said firmly. "I did him a favor by not sending him to the arena when I was Empress of the Villa the first week. We can cash in on that favor and get him to do something for us in return."

"And if that doesn't work?"

"You'll fight," I said. "If Pierce and Octavia work together, then yes, you'll be the underdog. I won't lie and say otherwise. But people love when an underdog wins. It's entertaining. And isn't that what the Faerie Games are all about? Entertainment?"

"Yes," she said slowly. "I guess."

"We haven't had a good underdog fight yet," I said. "I'd say it's about time for one. So who knows—maybe the arena will be designed in your favor."

"I hope so." She gave me a small smile, but I could tell it was forced. "Thanks for the chat. But if you don't mind, I'd like some time alone right now."

"Of course." I stood up from the bed. "Come find me if you need me, okay?"

"Okay." She snuggled under the covers again, curling up and pulling them to her chin. "Thanks for being such a great friend, Selena. And if this week doesn't go well, I want you to know that I hope you win."

TORRENCE

WE GATHERED around the map spread out on the table.

"Circe's island isn't far from here." Thomas traced the route with his finger. "Forty-five minutes, tops. I'll stop the boat until we come up with a plan to get her staff."

The engine turned off, and we stopped moving.

"Look at us, possibly getting two of the objects in one day." Sage sat back and smiled. "We'll be in the Otherworld before we know it."

"Let's not get cocky," Thomas said. "Circe's not a run-of-the-mill monster. She's an immortal sorceress. She's stronger than witches *and* mages. Stealing her staff will be difficult."

"We have the moly so we can resist her magic," I said, referring to the herb Odysseus had used in *The Odyssey* to do just that. Luckily, my mom had just about every herb in the Devereux apothecary—including moly. "So we're off to a good start."

"Perhaps we should continue taking an example from Odysseus," Thomas said. "Odysseus pulled his sword on Circe, and she invited him to bed with her. Once Circe's asleep, Reed can steal the staff, and we can hightail it out of there."

"Me?" Reed looked appalled.

"In every account of Circe, she's described as incredibly beautiful," Thomas said. "Spending a night with her surely wouldn't be the worst thing in the world."

"If that's what you think, then why don't you do it?" he asked.

"Because I'd never betray my mate." Thomas scooted closer to Sage and reached for her hand under the table.

"And I'd never betray my betrothed." Reed stared him down in challenge.

"Betrothed?" I tilted my head and studied Reed, jealousy coursing through me. "You mean you have a *fiancée?*"

"I haven't kept it a secret that I have someone waiting for me on Mystica," he said.

"I thought you had a girlfriend. Not a fiancée." The word felt strange on my tongue. Reed was seventeen. Who got engaged at seventeen? Was that even legal?

"You're jealous," he said simply.

"No." I bristled. "Why would I be jealous?"

Reed didn't bother answering the question. Instead, he stared at me, his expression indecipherable.

Before today, he would have said a sarcastic, snarky comment.

Something had definitely changed between us since we did that spell. And as much as he was denying it, I had a gut feeling that he felt it, too.

"Well." Sage smiled brightly, breaking the tension between the two of us. "Whoever stole your heart in Mystica must be a lucky girl."

"It's not like that," he said. "The princess and I have been betrothed since we were children."

Great. He's not just engaged, but he's engaged to a princess. How much worse can this get?

I couldn't even look at him. He'd humiliated me enough for one day. And that was saying a lot, because I wasn't the type to let a guy get to me so much.

I wished Reed had never been assigned to this quest with us in the first place.

"So it's a political arrangement," Thomas surmised.

"It is." Reed nodded. "Not only will the marriage benefit my family, but I've known the princess for as long as I can remember. She's one of my closest friends. I won't dishonor her by having a one-night stand with a sorceress, no matter how bewitching this sorceress is rumored to be."

"You don't love her?" The words came out of my mouth before I could stop them.

He froze, but quickly got ahold of himself. "I respect her, and I value our friendship," he said. "But no, I don't love her. At least not in the romantic sense."

"And she knows this?"

"She feels the same way about the betrothal as I do," he said. "Why the sudden interest in the politics of Mystica?"

Because the thought of you marrying someone you don't love makes me feel sick. You deserve better.

"As I'm sure you've seen during your time on Avalon, your customs are very different from what we're used to," Sage cut in. "A little curiosity is to be expected."

"It's how things have always been done amongst the noble families in Mystica." He straightened, looking proud of his realm's medieval ways. "The only exception would be..." His eyes locked on mine, leaving me breathless. But he didn't continue.

"The only exception would be what?" I asked.

"Never mind." He waved off the question. "It's unimportant, and we've gotten off subject."

"I was just about to bring us back around to the topic at hand," Thomas said, and all eyes went to him. "While the three of you were chatting, I've been thinking. Since seducing Circe isn't an option, perhaps we should go about this the old fashioned way."

"What way is that?" I asked.

"Launch a surprise attack, kill Circe, and take her staff," he said, as if it should have been obvious.

"I was thinking the same thing," Sage said.

I looked back and forth between the two of them in shock. "You can't be serious," I said, although it was clear from their expressions that they were.

"I know that killing Circe will be difficult," Thomas said. "Especially because like I said earlier, she's powerful. But there's one of her, and four of us. If we catch her unaware, there's no reason why we shouldn't be able to pull this off."

"That's not what I meant," I said.

"So what's the problem?"

"The problem is that Circe's not a mindless monster, or a demon with no conscience," I said. "She's a person. We can't kill her in cold blood. That goes against everything we're taught on Avalon."

Sage turned to me, her eyes tender. "On Avalon, we're taught not to kill innocents," she said. "But Circe's not an innocent. She's been turning the men who stumble onto her island into animals for thousands of years. By doing so, she's all but killed them. Putting an end to Circe will save any men who stumble upon her island in the future."

"And getting her staff will give us a chance to save Selena," Reed added. "That *is* why we're here, isn't it?"

"Of course it is." I narrowed my eyes at him, annoyed at him for doubting me—and annoyed at him for knowing the exact right thing to say to get me on board with killing Circe.

"Fine." I turned to Thomas. "How exactly should we go about this surprise attack?"

"I'm glad you asked," he said, and from there, he told us the plan.

SELENA

PIERCE WAS one of those people who was constantly surrounded by others at all times.

There was no way to talk to him without at least one person from his side knowing. So the day before the arena battle, I picked the time when I wouldn't have to deal with Octavia and Antonia, too.

Early morning, when Pierce did his daily workout with Emmet.

As always, the two guys were out in the backyard soon after the sun rose. I'd never been a morning person, but Cassia had no problem forcing me out of bed. We had a mission, and I was ready to help Cassia convince Pierce to work with her.

Emmet hovered over Pierce, holding his feet down for sit-ups, when Cassia and I walked outside. Emmet was muscular, but he looked small in comparison to Pierce, whose arms and legs were as wide as tree trunks.

His bulkiness made him heavy, which could easily be used against him in a fight.

I stepped on as many twigs and crunchy leaves as possible as Cassia and I walked over to them. Pierce jumped up when he saw us approaching, and Emmet followed his lead.

Pierce's eyes flashed with guilt. Then suspicion.

Emmet rubbed his hands together to brush off the dirt. "What brings you two lovely ladies out here so early?" he asked, smiling as we continued toward them.

Pierce was as still as a statue, and he said nothing.

"We need to speak with Pierce," Cassia said. "Alone."

"Finally." Emmet winked at Cassia. "I'm glad you're not giving up."

"No one's giving up." I focused on Pierce, waiting for him to answer.

"All right." He nodded. "I'll hear you out."

"That's my cue," Emmet said. "I was just about ready to wash up, anyway." He jogged over to the bathhouse, leaving the three of us alone in the backyard.

"Let's sit?" I motioned to a group of stumps nearby.

Pierce silently led the way and sat down. Cassia and I followed his lead and sat on two stumps across from him. The fall air was crisp, the birds chirped happily, and the tops of the stumps were damp with morning dew.

"Get out with it before the others wake up," Pierce said.

That was one thing I liked about Pierce. He was always quick to get to the point.

"When I was Empress of the Villa, I respected your wishes and didn't send you to the arena," I said. "By now, it's no secret that Julian and I are working together. And when he was Emperor of the Villa, he didn't send you to the arena, either."

"I have no grievances against you or Julian," Pierce said. "If you came out here to confirm that, then consider it confirmed." He tilted his head in Cassia's direction. "But none of that addresses why she's here."

Cassia straightened her shoulders and held Pierce's gaze. "I want you to work with me tomorrow to take out Octavia," she said.

"I figured as much," he said. "So why not come out here alone? Why bring Selena?"

I balled my fists, breathing slowly to calm the sparks of anger flaring through me. Pierce might look like a meathead, but he wasn't dense, like Emmet.

He just wanted us to admit to our alliance out loud.

"You were right the first week when you guessed that Cassia, Julian, and I are working together," I said.

"And when I was Empress of the Villa, you told me that if I didn't send you to the arena, you'd return the favor."

"I said I'd return the favor if I was Emperor of the Villa," he corrected me.

"Yes." I nodded, since I remembered that as well as he did. "But perhaps we could alter the agreement."

"I'm listening."

I took a deep breath. This was it. The biggest trump card I had to play. "If you work with Cassia in the arena tomorrow to take out Octavia, I'll consider us even."

He was silent for a few seconds. "An interesting proposition," he finally said. "But Octavia didn't send me to the arena when she was Empress of the Villa, either. Why should I fight against her when she's done me a favor, and Cassia has done nothing for me?"

"Because Octavia's the biggest threat in the Games," Cassia took over.

"That's debatable." Pierce glanced over at me.

"Octavia's taken out two champions so far, and she enjoyed both of those kills." Cassia didn't back down. "That makes her the biggest threat."

"Like I said, that's debatable."

"Fine," Cassia said. "But we both know she's far more of a threat than I am." He didn't argue with that, so she continued, "Work with me to take her out, and that's one fewer champion standing in your way of winning the Games."

The corner of his lips tilted up into a small smile.

Were we getting through to him?

"This is a bigger request than when I asked you not send me to the arena the first week," he said to me. "Unless you, Cassia, and Julian are offering a final four?"

My heart stopped, and I froze.

That came out of nowhere.

But I had to say something. Quickly. Before he took the option off the table.

"Yes," I lied. "We could do that."

"Cassia?" He looked to her.

I looked to her, too. *Lie*, I thought. *Forget about the deal with Felix. Lie to Pierce to save your life.*

"Unless you're still with Felix..." he said, confirming my suspicion that Octavia had told the others what she'd overheard in the sauna.

Cassia's wings shimmered at the mention of Felix's name. "Felix has been parading around with Antonia all week," she said. "I'm not stupid. I know what they're doing up there in her suite every night."

"So you're not with him anymore."

"No," she said, so strongly that I wondered if she was telling the truth.

She hadn't said anything to me about Felix since the

selection ceremony. And he was still keeping up the charade with Antonia, assumedly to infiltrate the other side of the house.

Maybe she'd finally had enough?

Pierce looked back and forth between the two of us. "Your points all make sense," he said. "And a final four with three strong players is tempting."

"So you're in?" I asked.

"I'll mull it over," he said. "But this was a good talk. You've given me a lot to consider."

Cassia moved forward to sit on the edge of the stump. "When will you let us know your decision?" she asked.

He smiled wickedly—a smile that reminded me of Bacchus's—and said, "You'll know my decision when you see whose side I take tomorrow in the arena."

TORRENCE

CIRCE'S ISLAND was next to a popular tourist destination called Pig Island.

"No one knows for sure how the pigs got to Pig Island," Thomas said as we passed the island packed with tourists swimming with the pigs. He, Sage, and I stood on deck. Reed was downstairs, brewing the moly tea. "Although there are many rumors. Many say they were dropped off by sailors who wanted to cook them but never returned, or that they survived a shipwreck, or that they were planted there to generate business as a tourist destination. Only a few guess the correct reason —that they escaped from a nearby islet."

"Aeaea," I said, recalling the name on the map. "Circe's island."

"Yes." He guided the yacht around Pig Island and toward one that appeared uninhabited.

The water around it was bright, sky blue, and it led to pristine white sand beaches lined with wild bushes and trees. Birds flew overhead, but other than that, the island was devoid of life.

"I don't see any pigs," Sage said.

"This was the island on the map," I said. "They have to be here."

Thomas sailed the yacht around the entire island. There were no pigs to be found.

"We should get off the yacht," I said once we were back where we'd started. "Explore a little."

Thomas dropped the anchor, and we went downstairs to the kitchen, where Reed was pouring the cups of moly tea. We drank it quickly—it was sweet and milky, with a slightly bitter aftertaste—and went downstairs to change.

I put on a bikini, a sheer white cover-up dress, and flip-flops. Then I wrapped a dagger in my towel, covering it completely.

Once changed, we boarded the motorboat at the back of the yacht. It was the first time I'd seen Thomas in something other than a suit. He looked more relaxed than ever in his swim trunks, t-shirt, and aviator sunglasses.

He sat in the captain's chair and leaned back, not needing to touch the steering wheel to drive us to the beach. "You have no idea how great it is to not worry about the sun draining me on Earth," he said as he soaked in the rays.

"One of the best perks of mating with me and becoming half shifter." Sage walked behind him and wrapped her arms around his neck.

"I can think of a few better ones." He tilted his head back to look up at her and smiled. "But yes, this one's up there."

We were nearly at the beach when a tingling sensation passed through me. My vision blurred for a second or two. It cleared, and the beach was no longer deserted.

It was full of pigs.

The pigs were swimming, walking around on the beach, and lying on the sand enjoying the sun. Some of them swam up to our boat, greeting us as we pulled up to the island. They oinked and smiled, and I reached down to pet one. He nuzzled up against my hand.

"You know those are actually men." Reed frowned. "They're not real pigs."

"I don't care," I said, petting another one. "They're cute."

Thomas anchored the boat at the end of the cove, where it could be partially hidden. We took off our flip-flops, grabbed our towels, and waded through the water to the beach. The water was as warm as a bathtub, which was a far cry from the cold ocean in LA.

"Circe's lair can't be far from here," Thomas said. "We'll wander until we find it."

"Or we can try something else." The first pig I'd petted had followed us to the shore, and I kneeled down to pet him again. "Hey there," I said. "Can you lead us to Circe?"

The pig turned its head up and snorted. Then it turned and trotted along the beach, its curly tail bouncing with each step.

I walked alongside him. The others followed, too.

We must have walked half a mile before we heard beautiful singing. It had to be Circe. Her voice grew louder as we turned into a cove lined with a small cliff. Smack in the middle of the cliff was a cave, and the singing was coming from inside of it.

Two lions were lying down on each side of the entrance.

We paused in our tracks. Thomas and Sage were strong in their wolf forms, but lions were stronger. And it was too early to blow our cover.

Sage kept her eyes trained on the lions. "They look pretty docile," she said as one of them licked its paw.

The other rolled over, stood up, and strolled toward us.

Reed held his hands out, ready to shoot out his magic.

"Stand down," Sage said to him, and he looked at her like she was crazy. "The lion's showing no signs of wanting to attack. And look into its eyes. They're almost *magical*, don't you think?"

I looked in the lion's eyes and saw what she meant. There was an otherworldly shimmer to them.

The lion approached Sage and nuzzled its nose into her side. She reached forward and stroked its neck, and the lion purred.

"See?" she said. "They're friendly."

It was a good thing we were wearing our cloaking rings. I wasn't sure how friendly the big cats would be if they smelled that Sage and Thomas were wolf shifters.

After a bit more petting, the lion turned to the cave and motioned for us to follow. The pig rubbed its nose against the back of my leg. He also looked at the cave—he was telling me to go inside of it.

"I guess this is where we part ways," I said, leaning down to give his head a final pet. "Thanks for helping us out."

He snorted, turned around, and trotted back to where we'd come from.

The lion led us to the cave, stopping once he reached his perch on the side of it. The other lion looked at us for a second and laid its head back down on the sand.

We looked at each other, nodded, and followed the singing into the cave.

25

SELENA

THE ARENA WAS AN ICE RINK, with three igloos on triangular points along the edges. But they didn't have little tunnel entrances like typical igloos. They were transparent ice brick domes, with no way in or out. A single ice pick sat inside of each one.

Curse the gods.

They'd designed this arena against Cassia. And while Pierce's fire could melt ice, the arena was clearly built in Octavia's favor.

"How can the gods and the fae *want* Octavia to win?" I said to Julian, who was sitting beside me in the Royal Box.

"Octavia's twisted." His eyes were hard as he looked ahead at the rowdy crowd. "They feed off of twisted."

"I guess that means they hate me."

"They also like surprises." He turned to me and gave my hand a small squeeze. "You being chosen by Jupiter —and the two of us being... well, the two of us—are definitely surprises."

"Then hopefully they'll like it when Cassia gives them a surprise today." I was trying to be positive, despite the pit of worry growing in my stomach.

"Hopefully," he said, although his tone was laced with doubt.

Pierce *needed* to come through for us.

I glanced over at Felix to see his reaction to the arena.

He leaned back in his chair, his legs crossed as he sipped a glass of honey wine. It was like he didn't care about the outcome of the fight at all.

Or he was an expert at hiding his emotions.

Either way, he was dangerous and not to be trusted.

Bacchus popped into the arena in an explosion of purple magic, ripping my attention away from Felix. He flew his chariot in circles while the crowd screamed his name.

The noise faded into the background as I prayed for Cassia to make it through this.

Bacchus slowed his chariot until he was floating midair in a sparkling purple cloud. "This challenge is relatively simple," he said. "Each champion had been given an ice pick. They must chip their way out of their igloo before the air runs out. The igloos had been strengthened by Neptune himself, to make them more difficult to escape. But don't worry—Neptune didn't know who would be in each igloo, so he couldn't give his chosen champion an advantage. Then, once they're out—*if* they get out—they'll fight each other. The first champion who's killed, or who suffocates inside the igloo, will be out of the Games!"

I stiffened as I looked at the claustrophobic igloos.

This isn't fair.

"Who's ready to see the chosen champions of Neptune, Vulcan, and Ceres fight to the death?" Bacchus's voice boomed through the arena, and the crowd exploded into hoots and applause. "I know there's a lot of anticipation surrounding this round," he continued. "So I won't delay any longer. Let the fight begin!"

Puffs of purple magic filled the insides of the igloos. The magic quickly faded, revealing Cassia, Octavia, and Pierce inside of them.

Cassia flung her green magic at the wall, but it did nothing. She scowled and lowered herself to the ground, pressing her hands to the ice at her feet. Her green wings glowed with the sign that she was harnessing magic. But again, nothing. So she grabbed the ice pick and started chipping away.

Pierce gathered flames in his hands, held out his palms, and shot giant blazes of fire straight ahead. The fire melted the ice, creating a door-sized opening. He ran through it, with seconds to spare before the igloo could no longer support itself and the ice bricks tumbled inward.

At the same time, Octavia's blue magic swirled around her, filling the igloo. The ice melted and turned to water, retaining its igloo form. It morphed and water spun around her, like it was a hurricane and she was the eye. Her dark ponytail whipped against her cheeks. Her ocean blue wings sparkled and shined, and she grinned at the cheering crowd.

Come on, Pierce, I thought. *Run to Cassia while Octavia's showing off. Get her out of that igloo.*

He looked back and forth between Octavia, who was still relishing in the storm of water spinning around her, and Cassia, who was only a quarter way done chipping through the dome of ice.

He ran halfway across the arena, fire building in his hands as he prepared to shoot it toward Cassia's igloo.

Yes. I held my breath in anticipation. *Set Cassia free. Then the two of you can attack Octavia together.*

Suddenly, the water crashed down around Octavia. It spread out in a thin sheet and turned back to ice. "Wait," she said to Pierce, and he stopped in his tracks. As always, her voice was magically amplified so everyone in the arena could hear. "Let's see how long it takes her to escape. That is, *if* she can escape at all."

Pierce turned away from Octavia to look at Cassia, pity in his eyes as he watched her put more force into each swing of the ice pick. The balls of fire blazed in his hands.

Now was the time to strike. He could use one hand to hold off Octavia, and his other to free Cassia.

But he looked back at Octavia, and the pity was gone, replaced by cold calculation.

"All right." The fireballs in his hands extinguished. "But try anything against me, and I won't hold back."

"Don't worry, Pyro," she said, although her eyes were on Cassia, who was halfway done chipping through the ice. "You're not the one I want out this week."

They walked toward Cassia's igloo, watching her calmly.

"No." My grip on Julian's hand tightened. "He can't do this."

I wasn't sure if Cassia could hear them through the ice. But she struck faster and faster, breathing heavily as she put all the force she could muster into each swing of the ice pick.

She didn't get much farther before her strikes slowed, the blows weakening. She paused, rested the ice pick on the ground, and leaned against it. Her eyes darted around, looking at the crowd like she was a bird trapped in a cage. Her wings were a much duller green than normal.

She raised the ice pick again, but wobbled while swinging it. It missed the spot she was working on, hitting half a foot off to the side.

It took all of her strength to pull the pick out of the ice. Her chest heaved, her arms shaking as she tried raising it above her head to keep going.

Her desperate eyes met mine, and she fell to the ground on her knees. The ice pick clattered down beside her.

Julian sat perfectly still and stared straight ahead.

"Pierce isn't going to save her," I said softly. "Is he?"

"No," he said, and the word was a blow to my heart.

Cassia was sitting down now, her hands flat on the ground behind her. Her mouth was open, her breaths shallow as she struggled to breathe. The green light of her wings flickered in and out.

She leaned her head back, closed her eyes, and smiled.

"Death by gradual suffocation isn't painful," Julian said, his voice low. "Right now, it looks like she feels high. Soon, she'll fall asleep, and then, she'll pass peacefully."

"No," I said again. "There's still time. Pierce can still save her."

The crowd was silent, waiting with bated breath as they watched the light dim in Cassia's wings.

Octavia took a few steps forward, raising her hands as her blue magic swirled around them. Her wings shined brighter than ever. "You don't think I'm letting this fight end *that* easily, do you?" she asked.

She shot her magic toward the igloo, and the ice blocks collapsed inward, crashing down on Cassia and crushing her in their frozen embrace.

26

SELENA

COLD REALIZATION FLOODED MY BONES.

Cassia was gone.

Everyone in the arena—including Octavia and Pierce—looked up to Bacchus, waiting for him to call it.

The god smirked, saying nothing.

People in the crowd pointed into the center of the arena. I followed their fingers to the pile of ice bricks that used to be Cassia's igloo.

Green light glowed from under them. The light was dim, but it was there.

My breath caught in my throat. Cassia was still alive.

Octavia rubbed her hands together and smiled. "This is gonna be more fun than I expected." She straightened her arms, palms out, and shot more blue magic toward the pile.

The ice blocks melted into water, flowing outward to reveal Cassia's crushed, mangled body.

Her arms and legs were splayed out, bent in unnatural directions. Her hands were trapped in orbs of ice, blocking her from using her magic. Her eyes were open, staring upward as she took in shallow, pained breaths.

She opened her mouth to speak, but all that came out were strained croaks.

My heart dropped. I leaned into Julian, and he wrapped his arm around my shoulders, pulling me closer. I didn't want to watch—I didn't want to see Cassia like this.

But I couldn't look away.

Any hope that Cassia could get out of this alive was squelched. All I wanted was for her to be put out of her misery.

The orbs buzzed around her, broadcasting a close-up of her face on the screen as a single tear escaped her eye and froze midway down her cheek.

"Stand back," Octavia said to Pierce. "This kill is mine."

His stare was heavy. "Remember that her family's watching," he said. "Whatever you do, do it quickly."

"And ruin the fun?" She raised an eyebrow and laughed. "Why would I do that?" She strutted toward Cassia, kneeled down beside her, and hovered over her to look her in the eyes. "Hi there, Baby Bird," she said, the end of her long dark ponytail grazing Cassia's chest. "You thought you got one over on me, didn't you? Back there in the sauna. You really believed that Felix would choose you over me."

Cassia whimpered, another tear rolling down her face and freezing on her cheek.

Octavia flicked the frozen drop away. "I knew about you and Felix from the beginning." She smiled wickedly. "He told me every last, boring detail each time he came to me so I could give him what you couldn't."

More tears, coming faster now, freezing into puddles of ice on Cassia's cheeks. Her skin underneath them was a bright, angry red.

I glanced over at Felix.

He downed the last of his wine. A half-blood servant stepped up from the back of the box and offered to pour him more. He accepted.

The entire time, his expression was blank. Uncaring. Distant.

Like he wasn't there at all.

Traitor.

Then, he looked at me. His face crumpled, his eyes flashed with agony, and his pink wings darkened.

"She's lying," he mouthed to me. He took another sip

of wine, and it washed away all his emotion. He looked straight ahead again.

But I'd seen him, in that split second. He was hurting just as much as I was.

I swallowed down a lump in my throat and refocused on the center of the arena.

Octavia sat back into her heels and trailed her fingers down Cassia's arm. Once she reached the sphere of ice around her hand, she picked it up and cradled it.

"Such pretty, perfect, soft hands," she said. "The hands of someone who's never done a hard day's work in her life."

Some of the ice melted, exposing Cassia's fingers but still blocking her palms. Octavia took Cassia's pinky and caressed it.

Then she ripped the nail straight off.

Cassia let out a strained, strangled gasp, and I buried my face in Julian's shoulder.

But I forced myself to look again.

Octavia moved on to rip off the nail on Cassia's ring finger. Electricity roared under my skin.

But I had control over my magic now. It would only strike when *I* wanted it to.

So I sat straighter and stopped leaning into Julian's comforting arm. I wasn't going to miss a single second.

Because the more I saw, the more rage I'd have to throw at Octavia when I finally got to kill her.

Octavia moved on, finger by finger, ripping the nail off of each one. A dim, green light glowed in Cassia's palms—her magic. But Octavia's blue magic surrounded the spheres of ice and extinguished the green.

"Trying to put up a fight against my own element?" Octavia chucked. "That's cute."

Once Octavia finished with Cassia's first hand, she moved onto the second. She placed each nail down next to her after ripping it off Cassia's fingers, handling them delicately to create a neat little pile on the ice.

After all ten nails were gone, she arranged Cassia's hands on her chest. The raw, bloodied nail beds faced up for everyone to see. "Much better." She smiled at her work. "Now your hands aren't perfect anymore. But we're not done yet."

She moved on to Cassia's feet and ripped the nails off every one of her toes. Thin, icy crystals covered Cassia's skin. Frozen sweat.

I held onto Julian's hand so tightly that I was surely drawing blood.

Cassia's eyes were closed now, tears still running out of them.

Octavia ripped off the final toenail, looked at the little mounds of frozen tears collecting on Cassia's cheeks, and shook her head. "So weak," she said. "I can't listen to any more of your pathetic crying." She crawled to Cassia's head, hovered over her face, and curved her index finger into a hook. "Cassia," she sung each syllable of my sweet friend's name. "Look at me."

No. Don't open your eyes.

She did.

Octavia dug her finger into Cassia's eye, so deep that she had to be touching the back of it.

Cassia's back arched. Her hands surrounded by ice thudded to the ground as she let out strained, strangled screams. Goosebumps prickled over my skin, her cries like nails on a chalkboard as they echoed through the silent arena.

Even the fae were horrified by Octavia's brutality.

Octavia held Cassia's shoulder down with her other hand, digging with her finger until she scooped Cassia's eyeball out of its socket with a sickening squish.

She held it in front of her, smiled at it, and tossed it over her shoulder. It rolled a few times and stopped.

An orb buzzed around it, enlarging the misshapen, bloodied sphere on the screen for everyone to see. Half of Cassia's familiar green iris stared out at me. But I still didn't look away.

Instead, I turned back to the two of them.

Cassia was squeezing her remaining eye shut.

Octavia pried it open with her other hand. Her index finger was covered with blood and mucus, and she lowered it slowly, hovering it in front of Cassia's eye.

"It's only fitting," she said with another wicked smile. "That I'm the last face you'll ever see."

"ENOUGH!" Pierce ran forward with his ice pick and shoved Octavia to the side.

Time slowed. Hope rose within me.

He's going to kill Octavia.

But he raised the weapon over his head and swung the blade down into Cassia's chest.

My heart shattered at the same time as hers.

She sucked in a strangled breath, shuddered, and stilled.

Octavia stood and spun to face Pierce. Icicles grew from the ground like crystal stalagmites around her. "That was *my* kill," she raged, her hands balled into fists. "And you're going to pay for taking it from me."

Her blue magic spiraled around her, tiny ice crystals sparkling inside of it.

Pierce towered over her, not moving. The thick veins in his muscles throbbed. He held her gaze in challenge.

She snarled and took a few steady breaths. The magic around her dimmed, although she still stared at Pierce with hate and rage and *murder* in her eyes.

"Champions!" Bacchus landed next to them, his

jovial voice out of place in the dark arena. But there was an edge of something else in his tone. *Warning.*

Octavia reined her magic back in.

Pierce stood as strong as ever, glaring at the god.

Bacchus looked away from them, grinned at the crowd, and held up his arms. "The fight is over!" He was met with hesitant applause, although it slowly grew louder. "Cassia—the chosen champion of Ceres—has been defeated. Her soul is on its way to Elysium, where she'll be honored as a goddess for all eternity." He spun in a slow circle to take in everyone in the arena, and continued, "May her crossing to the Underworld be a peaceful one!"

"May her crossing to the Underworld be a peaceful one!" the crowd repeated.

My eyes stayed on Cassia's mangled, reddened, tortured body.

As I stared at her, something deep within me broke.

"It's you and me now," I said to Julian, my voice darker than I'd ever heard it before. "And we're going to kill them all."

27

TORRENCE

WE DIDN'T HAVE to walk long before reaching the cave's exit. It led out to a huge circular space surrounded by cliffs at least five times my height. With our supernatural strength, we'd easily be able to scale the cliffs. Humans wouldn't stand a chance.

In the center of the circle, wide steps led up to a pristine marble palace surrounded by floor to ceiling columns. Wolves prowled the base of the steps. A woman with long dark hair sat at the top, singing as she wove colorful threads through a gigantic loom.

Circe.

She stopped singing, turned to us, and grabbed something that had been resting by her side.

A golden staff.

She stood and adjusted her tiara. In her yellow and

blue draping gown, she looked like a goddess from the storybooks. "Welcome, travelers," she said with a smile. "What brings you to my humble abode?"

I stifled a laugh. The palace behind her could hardly be described as *humble*.

"We were supposed to meet our tour guide on the island," Reed said sheepishly. "But we can't find anyone anywhere. Then we heard your singing and followed it here. We were hoping you could help us."

"The tour company's called Exuma's Excellent Adventures," Sage piped in. "Have you heard of it?"

"Ah, of course," Circe said. "I'm afraid you're early. They won't be here for another hour or so. Why don't you come inside and join me for a late lunch while you wait?"

She had to be lacing her words with magic. No one in their right mind would believe it was too early for the tours to have started.

"That would be amazing." I smiled and held tighter to my towel. "I'm starving."

We climbed the steps and followed her through a magnificent hall. "I'm Circe," she said as she opened the doors to a surprisingly cozy dining room. "I've lived on this island since way before it became a tourist destination."

"You have a lovely home," I said with a hopefully vapid smile.

"Thank you, my dear." She motioned to the cushioned chairs. "Please, have a seat. I'll be back with your meals in a moment."

We sat down, placing our towels close by our sides.

Five minutes later, Circe wheeled in a trolley with five bowls of soup, spoons, and glasses of wine. The soup was dark yellow with chunks of vegetables, and smelled delicious. She gripped her staff in one hand the entire time.

It was so tempting to make a go for the staff right then. But we needed to catch her as unaware as possible. Which meant waiting until she thought we were drunk on her magic.

"Pottage of cheese stew," she said as she placed a bowl in front of each of us. A sweet scent of magic that smelled like honey drifted up from it. "My specialty."

Circe placed the final bowl at the head of the table, sat down, and we all dug in.

The moly better work, I thought as I lifted the spoon to my mouth and took my first bite.

The stew tasted as good as it smelled. Judging by the others' sounds of approval, they agreed.

The four of us introduced ourselves, and we spent the meal telling Circe about our pretend vacation yachting through the Bahamas. It was easy to make up the details, and she didn't appear to question any of it. We barely touched the wine, but as we ate we pretended to be drunker and drunker, assuming the magic would affect us in a similar way as alcohol.

Sage lifted the bowl to her lips once she'd reached the bottom and drank the last of it down. The rest of us followed suit.

Circe placed her spoon down in her empty bowl. "I'm glad you enjoyed the stew," she said. "Now, for the best part. My homemade dessert wine." She smiled again, stood up with her staff, and placed our dirty dishes back on the trolley. Then she turned to leave the room.

The moment her back was toward us, Reed jumped out of his chair and shot a blast of yellow magic straight at her. Sage and Thomas shifted into wolves, and I grabbed my dagger, ready to back them up if necessary.

Circe spun and blasted deep gold magic out of the top of her staff to hold off Reed's light yellow magic, at the same time as she used her other hand to create a force field that knocked Sage and Thomas to the ground mid-pounce. I ran forward to attack, but the tip of my knife crashed into a nearly transparent wall of gold magic.

She'd extended the force field to block me, too.

Reed grunted, beads of sweat forming on his brow as he pushed his magic against Circe's. But her darker, gold magic inched forward on his. Her dark hair floated around her, and she didn't seem to be struggling in the slightest.

I tried shooting out the mage magic I'd used to protect me from Scylla so I could help Reed.

Nothing happened.

With only millimeters of Reed's magic protecting him from Circe's blast, he braced himself to fight harder. But it was no use. Her magic overtook his and surrounded him in an orb of golden light.

He shimmered, turned to lock his eyes with mine, and disappeared. A pig stood in his place.

Circe dropped the force field that was blocking us, aimed her staff toward Thomas, and turned him into a pig, too.

Sage and I launched an attack. But the force field was back up in a second.

"I don't know what kind of sorcerers you are," Circe said, the earlier sweetness gone from her voice. "But I'm stronger than you. Stand down, or I'll slaughter your lovers and force you to eat them for dinner."

Sage shifted back into human form and held up her hands in defeat.

I placed my knife on the ground, stood back up, and did the same.

I didn't know if Circe turned women into pigs, too. But now wasn't the time to find out.

Circe nodded and lowered her force field. "I have questions for you," she said. "Let's sit back down. And don't try anything else against me. I'm a woman who sticks to my word, and the lives of your lovers mean nothing to me."

"Reed's not my lover," I said.

"Please. I saw how you looked at him," she said. "Deny it all you want, but you yearn for him deeply."

I pressed my lips together, my cheeks heating as I looked at the pig that used to be Reed. Once he and Thomas were changed back and we were sailing away from here with Circe's staff, he was definitely going to give me hell for that.

But attacking clearly wasn't going to work against Circe. Sage and I needed to stall while we came up with another angle of approach.

So if Circe wanted to talk, then fine. We'd talk.

Sage must have been thinking the same thing, because she walked with me back to the table, and we took our seats.

Circe returned to her spot at the head of the table.

"No need to fetch the dessert wine," she said. "The boys were going to have a special brew that turned them to swine, although as we all know, that's already been accomplished." She glanced proudly at the pigs, who were oinking behind me. "The two of you were going to get one that relaxed you further, so we could enjoy ourselves on the island together. Then I'd erase your memories of your time here and send you on your way. Although I doubt it would have worked, since you resisted the potion in the stew. So, tell me. How did you do it?" She leaned back, like she had all the time in the world to wait for our answer.

Which, as an immortal sorceress, she did.

She can't know about the moly, I thought. *If she does, she'll use her potions on us once the moly's out of our systems. Which means...*

"We're supernaturals," I said quickly, not wanting Sage to have the chance to tell her the truth. "Being supernatural makes us immune to your potions."

I didn't know if it was a lie or the truth.

I just knew I didn't want to find out. And Circe had already seen that we weren't human, so there was no point in lying about it.

Judging by the way Sage nodded in agreement, she felt the same way.

Circe's eyes narrowed in suspicion. "Supernaturals

don't know about the ancient immortals living beside them on Earth," she said. "They believe our kind to be myths. If you are what you claim, you shouldn't have been able to stumble upon—let alone *see*—my island. Yet, here you are. And I want to know how."

28

TORRENCE

"WE DIDN'T KNOW that the myths were true until a few days ago." Sage didn't even pause before answering. "And it seems like just knowing has ruined our vacation." She huffed and leaned back in her chair.

So, we're still going with that story.

"How, exactly, did you discover that the myths are true?" Circe tilted her head, not looking like she believed us.

She couldn't know the truth. Then she'd surely turn us into pigs on the spot—and probably eat all four of us for dinner.

We needed another story. And the best lies were based on the truth.

Here goes nothing.

"My mom forced me to do some cataloging in our

archives." I rolled my eyes, like I did whenever I was talking about a tedious school assignment. "It was punishment for... well, never mind. That's a long and boring story. But while I was cataloging, I came across a bunch of dusty old books about mythology in the children's section. I glanced through one, and it was about how all the myths are true."

"She brought them on our vacation to show us." Sage glared at me before turning her attention back to Circe. "That's what got us into this mess in the first place."

"It wasn't my fault." I raised my hands in defense.

"Um, yeah." Sage crossed her arms and glared at me again. "It was."

We sat there in a stare-down for a few seconds. Circe looked back and forth between us, like she was trying to decide if she believed our story.

"So, you ended up on my island by accident," she finally said.

"We were looking for Pig Island." I shrugged. "We saw pigs, and thought this was it."

"An understandable mistake." She tilted her head, still studying us. "But it doesn't explain how the calming magic of my lions affected you, yet my potion in the stew did nothing."

"I'm a wolf shifter," Sage said. "As is my mate, Thomas." She glanced at where his pig form was standing by her feet. "We're in tune with animals. We could easily tell that the lions weren't going to hurt us."

Circe twirled her staff lazily in her hand. "Your transformation into a wolf *was* impressive," she said, turning her attention to me. "But you didn't transform into an animal. What kind of supernatural are you?"

"I'm a witch." I squared my shoulders proudly. "I can cast spells and create potions."

"I'm familiar with witches," she said. "Some call me a witch, although I prefer the term sorceress."

"I guess sorceresses are similar to witches," I said, figuring now was a good time to throw in a compliment. "Although sorceresses are *far* more powerful."

"Clearly," she said with the hint of a smile.

Was our story actually working?

"What about your lover?" She glanced at the pig that was Reed. "Is he a witch, too?"

"Reed's not my type," I said, mostly for his benefit. "But he's a mage. Mages are stronger than witches. Although as you just saw, they're weaker than sorceresses." I smiled again. I was laying it on thick, but I'd say whatever was necessary to get her to turn the guys back to normal.

"Hm." Circe leaned back and crossed her legs, showing some skin through the slit of her dress. "This is all quite interesting. But none of it explains why you tried to kill me."

I froze, and the blood drained out of my face.

"We read about you," Sage quickly came to my rescue. "In Torrence's books. But we didn't put it together until we were in here eating."

"What tipped you off?" she asked.

"The pottage of cheese stew." Sage glanced at the bowls on the trolley. "You served Odysseus the same thing, right?"

"I did." She nodded.

"Well, maybe that stew was common in Odysseus's time," she continued. "But nowadays? Not so much. We had to stop to look it up while we were reading the story in the book. I guess it's one of those things you don't forget."

"So the soup tipped you off," she said slowly. "Not the pigs? Not the palace? Not my clothing? Not my staff?"

"Eccentric humans build mansions on small islands all the time." I waved off her questions. "Artists, celebrities, heiresses, politicians… you know the drill. They're into some strange stuff. But stew cooked for peasants? Definitely not their thing."

"Definitely not." Sage shook her head in agreement, and we looked at each other like we were trying not to laugh.

"Fine." Circe's cheeks flushed pink. "But you still haven't explained why you tried to kill me."

"We weren't trying to kill you," I said, like she was being silly. "We were just trying to incapacitate you so we could bolt before you could turn us to pigs and add us to your collection on the beach."

"A simple misunderstanding," Sage said. "We shouldn't have underestimated your power. But look on the bright side—you're so much more powerful than us that there was no harm done! So if you wouldn't mind turning Thomas and Reed back to normal, we'll just be on our way and continue our vacation."

Circe raised the top of her staff to her chin, like she was considering it.

Please, please, please work, I thought. *Then we can get back on the yacht and figure out a better plan for stealing the staff.*

"The two of you fascinate me." Her eyes roamed over my figure in a way that reminded me of King Devin. "I've never met a wolf shifter or a witch before. I'd like to know more about your kind."

"No problem." Sage smiled, although I could tell it was forced. "Once the guys are turned back to normal, we'll tell you whatever you want to know."

"Not so fast." Circe chuckled, her eyes roaming over Sage's body, too. "I don't trust men. At least, not anymore. I want to learn from the two of you. And Aeaea's a beautiful place for a vacation. Stay here for a while, and I'll make sure your every need is taken care of."

She said the last part like a promise.

Judging by the way she was checking out me and Sage, I had a feeling about what sort of "needs" she was referring to.

"This is actually our last day of vacation." I sighed, making sure to sound disappointed. "School starts up right when we get back. But Aeaea's the most beautiful island I've ever seen. I'd love to come back over winter break." I smiled in a way that I hoped was flirtatious. As I'd learned in the Tower, a little bit of flirting could go a long way.

"Yes." Sage sat straighter, brought her hands together, and batted her eyes at Circe. "That would be amazing."

"No can do," Circe said. "You're already here, and you've aroused my curiosity. School can wait. I can't."

"But you're an immortal sorceress." I laughed. "You have all the time in the world."

"Just because I'm immortal, it doesn't mean I'm patient." She pouted, her lips somehow still the perfect berry color they'd been before we'd eaten. "I'll transform your male companions back when I'm ready to send you on your way. You have my word. And I promise to make your time here more than worth your while."

She rested an elbow on the table, smiling as she pushed up her cleavage. It was impossible *not* to look.

There are worse things than a beautiful sorceress flirting with you, I told myself, doing my best to rationalize it. *There's no denying that Circe's attractive. And Thomas* had *mentioned flirting as a potential plan for stealing the staff...*

I hadn't considered that as something that would fall on Sage or me. But we needed that staff, we needed off this island, and we needed to do it quickly.

Our two best options right now seemed to be stealing the staff while Circe was sleeping and using it to change the guys back ourselves, or spending time with her so she'd change the guys back and let us leave so we could come up with another plan.

None of those sounded good to me.

Just because you don't like your options, it doesn't mean you don't have them, I could practically hear Selena's voice in my ear.

"I suppose we could stay for a night." I looked at Sage, as if asking her approval. "Right?"

"A night?" Circe gasped and pressed her palm to her chest. "That's not nearly enough time to show you all the splendor Aeaea has to offer."

"Oh." Sage frowned. "How long were you thinking?"

"A year, at the least," Circe said, and my heart dropped into my stomach.

"We can't stay for an entire *year*," I said.

"Why ever not?" Circe asked. "A year isn't that long. You'll enjoy yourselves so much that it'll pass in a blink."

"Maybe a year isn't long for an immortal like yourself," Sage replied gently. "But we have human lifespans."

It wasn't a lie, since if we lived on Earth instead of Avalon, we'd age like mortals. It was only Avalon's magic that kept us young forever.

"You misunderstand," Circe said sweetly. "I *insist* that you stay. Make any attempts to leave or go against me again before a year has passed, and I'll turn you into swine just like I did to your men."

Sage glanced to me, a familiar wolfish glint in her eyes.

It was time to play dirty.

I had no idea what our plan was yet, but we'd figure it out.

"I suppose you're right," I forced myself to say. "A year isn't *that* long in the scheme of things."

"That's more like it." Circe beamed. "I'm so honored to have two beautiful supernatural women as my guests. I'll give you the best rooms—apart from my own, of course."

"That's very kind of you." I met her smile with an equally sugary sweet one of my own.

"Like I said, this stay will be an enjoyable one." She pushed back her chair and stood up. "My home is your home. Now, follow me, and I'll help you get comfortable."

29

SELENA

IT HAD BEEN NEARLY three weeks, and there was still no word from Avalon. But I didn't let myself dwell on it. Whatever was happening on Earth was out of my control.

Instead, I focused on what I *could* control. Making sure Julian and I stayed alive.

The day after Cassia's death, Julian won Emperor of the Villa. He sent Octavia, Pierce, and Emmet to the arena. With Pierce and Emmet being so close, it seemed like a no brainer that they'd team up against Octavia. They were strong enough together to easily take her down.

Instead, Octavia and Emmet teamed up to take out Pierce. Octavia had the final blow. She enjoyed it nearly as much as she'd enjoyed torturing Cassia.

"Payback for taking my kill away from me last week!" she'd screamed as she held Pierce's heart up in the air, his blood dripping down her arm like war paint.

When I asked Emmet why he'd teamed up against his supposed best friend in the Games, his answer was simple.

He wouldn't be able to kill Pierce himself. So he figured it was best to have Octavia do it for him.

Next, Octavia won Empress of the Villa in a competition *clearly* designed in her favor. Her only options to send to the arena were me, Julian, Emmet, Felix, or Antonia. Emmet was the brawn working with her, and Felix wasn't a physical threat. Plus, Octavia bristled every time Felix got *near* Antonia.

So she sent Julian and me into the arena with Antonia.

Julian made Antonia's death as quick and painless as possible.

This week, I'd won Empress of the Villa. With only four other champions left in the Games including Julian, my decision might as well have been made for me.

Octavia, Emmet, and Felix.

Part of me wanted Emmet to take Octavia out.

Another part of me didn't, so I could do it myself.

However, I'd been preparing myself all week for the logical result. Octavia and Emmet would join forces against Felix. The two of them together would be much stronger against Julian and me when we had to duke it out next week.

I watched the fight with the same detachment as Sorcha, even when the final blow was struck.

"Emmet—the chosen champion of Mercury—is officially out of the Games!" Bacchus announced.

I barely heard the rest of it.

Because Octavia's heart had won out over her head.

And I couldn't wait to finally get my revenge.

SELENA

I ENTERED that bathhouse that afternoon, ready to clean up, when I found the last person I wanted to see.

Octavia.

She was in the bathtub, with bubbles all around her. They glowed from the light of her ocean blue wings. She was leaning her head over the edge, and her eyes were closed. It looked like she was sleeping.

She was usually in and out of the shower quickly so she could return to her alliance-mates. She always had *someone* by her side. Now that they were all gone, I supposed she didn't have to worry about anyone conspiring against her. She could finally be alone.

I turned and tiptoed back toward the door, hoping to leave before she noticed I was there.

"Selena," she said, stopping me in my tracks. "Trying to avoid me, are you?"

I spun back around. She'd raised her head, and was looking at me straight on.

"We've barely spoken for the entire Games," I said. "I have no intention of changing that now."

"No surprise there." She sat up, the bubbles just below her shoulders. "You think you're so much better than the rest of us, don't you?"

"No." I raised my chin.

"Liar."

"You're the one who's been parading around the house with your little minions from the beginning, like you'd won the Games already," I said. "But look around. Where are your minions now?"

"Dead." She shrugged. "Like you should be. But you just won't die, will you, Selena?" There was a singsong quality to her voice, and she actually *giggled*.

Octavia was losing it. The Games had taken a part of all of us, even for her.

But she hadn't started like this. At least I didn't think she had. And there was one big question I'd been burning to ask her...

"You've wanted me dead since day one," I said. "Why?"

"You have no idea what my life's been like." She

leaned forward in the tub, her eyes narrowed. "My father escaped this godforsaken city when I was seven years old. He was searching for a secret half-blood sanctuary—something from a story told to half-blood children to help us sleep at night. He said he would send for me and my mom once he found it." She gave a half-hearted laugh, and I knew what she was going to say before she said it. "We never heard from him again. Killed by the monsters in the North, most likely."

I didn't want to hear about Octavia's life. I didn't want to feel an inkling of sorrow for the girl who'd tortured my friend and enjoyed it.

But my feet were glued to the floor.

"Then there was my mother—my poor, weak mother." She smiled, like she was getting a kick out of telling me this. "It took her two years to realize my father wasn't coming back for us. She was never right in the head after that. She couldn't do much of anything, let alone keep a job. With her mind so useless, she used the only thing she could to keep a roof over our heads. Her body."

"She prostituted herself to the fae," I said.

"Not to the fae." Octavia laughed again. "My mother was no courtesan, at least not with her mind only half there. So she sold herself to half-bloods.

"Then, when I was eleven years old, she realized a

way she could make more money," she continued. "You see, men will pay a decent amount for a grown woman. But there are some out there with a much younger taste. They'd pay twice as much for a child. More if the child is a virgin."

Horror sank into my bones. "You didn't…"

"No." She let out a single laugh. "She brought him into my room. She told me to listen to him and do whatever he said. She left me alone with him. But the moment I realized what he was asking of me… what she wanted me to let him do to me…" She shuddered, like she was back there in that room, re-living each awful second. Then she snapped her focus back to me. "I killed him," she said. "When he was hovering over me, I grabbed my stylus off my nightstand and rammed it up his jaw. I stabbed him over and over and over again. I hated him, I hated my father for leaving me, and I hated my mother for trying to sell my body to the highest bidder. And each time I rammed that stylus into him—each time I left another bloody hole in his body—I felt better. Calmer. More in control. Just like I did when I took my time with your dear, sweet Cassia."

Whatever pity I felt for Octavia was squashed the moment she said Cassia's name.

"You enjoyed it," I said. "However many people you've killed, you enjoyed it every time. Haven't you?"

"You talk like you're so much better than me." She sneered. "But you're not. Or have you already forgotten what you did to Bridget?"

"That was different," I said, although my voice trembled when I said it.

"How so?"

I opened my mouth, but then closed it. Because how *was* it different? Did one death matter more than another because of how it was dealt out? At the end of the day, murder was murder. It was still one more person gone from the world before their time, at someone else's hand.

"We're not so different, after all." Octavia smirked. "Are we, Princess?"

I backed toward the door, needing to get out of that cramped, stuffy room.

"Don't you want to hear the rest?" Octavia asked. "Don't you want to know why I hate you so much?"

Angry electricity buzzed under my skin.

I wasn't angry at her for taunting me.

I was angry because she was right. I *did* want to know why she hated me. Because while everything she'd told me so far was awful, it still didn't answer my original question.

So I stayed where I was.

She smiled again, looking pleased with herself.

"Once he was dead—once I made that final hole in his heart—I packed up my satchel and left through the window," she continued. "I lived on the streets, on the other side of the city, where my mom wouldn't find me. Not that she ever came looking."

"I'm sorry," I said, since I truly was. Not for the Octavia I was looking at now, but for the child she'd once been.

"Then there's you." She ran her fingers through the bubbles, which were slowly disappearing in the tub. "Princess Selena. Raised by a king and queen in a castle on a utopian island, daughter of one of the most powerful princes in the Otherworld, and the first ever chosen champion of Jupiter. I hated you before we entered the villa. But you just won't die." The water crashed in small waves around her, splashing over the rim of the tub. "*Why* won't you die?"

"So that's what this all comes down to?" I flexed my fingers, ready to defend myself with my magic if she attacked. "Jealousy?"

"No." The water boiled around her, her cheeks flushed with rage. "It comes down to the fact that after everything I've been through—after all the hardships I've endured—I deserve to win. My entire life has prepared me for the Games. And I'm not going to let a spoiled little princess take that away from me. Especially now that my victory is so close I can taste it."

"You won't win," I said. "Maybe you could have if you'd kept Emmet instead of Felix. But now it's three against one. And you have no one to blame for that but yourself."

The water stopped boiling. Everything was eerily silent and still.

Octavia stood up, her eyes not leaving mine as the water slid off her naked body. "You really think Felix is on your side," she said. "Don't you?"

"He mourned Cassia more than I did," I said. "You saw him. *Everyone* saw him."

"He's a magnificent actor." She stepped out of the tub and slipped into her robe. "And I'm not so bad myself."

Tendrils of dread curled in my stomach. "What do you mean?" I asked slowly.

"You didn't think that little temper tantrum I threw in the sauna was real," she said as she tied the belt of her robe. "Did you?"

"You were jealous of Cassia." I stayed perfectly still, refusing to let Octavia get to me. "That's your fatal flaw. Jealousy. You're only saying it wasn't real to save face."

"Come *on*." She rolled her eyes. "That whole thing was planned. Didn't you or your boyfriend wonder how

I happened to be at the exact right place at the exact right time?"

"You were looking for Felix..." I said, although now that she'd said it, I realized she *did* have a point.

"Felix told me to be there," she said. "He wanted to put a rift in your little foursome. He's loyal to me, and he always has been."

"No." It took all my effort to stop my lightning from erupting from my palms. "He's loyal to us. He was loyal to *Cassia*."

"You really are gullible, aren't you?"

I didn't bother to reply. Instead, I headed to the door, opened it, and looked at Octavia over my shoulder. "Come on," I said.

Amusement danced in her eyes. "Where are we going?" she asked.

"To find Felix and Julian," I said. "It's time for the four of us to talk, so Felix can tell us the truth once and for all."

SELENA

I STORMED INTO THE VILLA, Octavia at my heels. The orbs buzzed behind us.

They want a show? Then I'll give them a show.

"JULIAN!" I yelled. "FELIX!" I went from room to room, throwing the doors open and screaming their names.

I found them in the game room playing *Latrunculi*—an ancient Roman form of chess.

"What happened?" Julian shot out of his chair and hurried to me. He skidded to a stop when he was a few feet away.

Why?

A glance at my hands showed me. Electricity danced across them, spreading over my body. I was a light bulb turned up to full wattage, and I was about to burst.

"I'm fine." I took a deep breath, and the magic fizzled out. "But Octavia and I just had an interesting chat in the bathhouse. The four of us need to talk. Now."

Julian was by my side in an instant. Octavia stood in front of the doors in her bathrobe, smirking and not saying a word.

Felix didn't bother getting up from his chair. "What kind of chat?" he asked.

"She says you *told* her to come to the sauna so she'd overhear us talking," I said. "That you've been loyal to her from the beginning."

Felix looked to Julian, to Octavia, and finally, to me.

Then, he laughed.

"No shit," he finally said. "It should have been obvious on day one, when she took me with her on that horse."

I froze, his easy admittance catching me off guard. "But the two of you didn't even know each other then," I said. "You were just taking what she offered. You were saving your own skin."

"That's what I wanted you to believe," he said. "But come on. Look at her." He motioned to Octavia, roaming his eyes appreciatively over her body. When he met her eyes again, they gave each other seductive smiles. "She's gorgeous. I'm gorgeous. We're perfect together. Why would I settle for anything but the best?"

"But Cassia..." Her name caught in my throat as Octavia sauntered over to Felix and made herself comfortable in his lap.

Felix wrapped his arm protectively around Octavia's waist. "Cassia was desperate for love," he said in disgust. "She *wanted* to be consumed by my magic. She didn't try to fight it—not even once. It was pathetic."

"But you loved her," I said. "You mourned her."

"I was pretending." He shrugged. "It was the perfect way to get protection from you and Julian. And hey—it worked."

"What did I tell you in the bathhouse?" Octavia looked to me as she ran her fingers across Felix's chest. "He's a *magnificent* actor."

Rage coursed through me, but I controlled it. I'd get my revenge in the arena.

Until then, the best way to fight was with words. And Felix was Octavia's weakness. His magic had clearly gotten to her, too.

I'd seen how hurt she'd been when she'd seen him with Cassia and Antonia.

I could use that to break her.

"He *is* a good actor." I agreed, focusing only on her. "But what if *you're* the one falling for it? Let's think about it, here. He used Antonia. He used Cassia." It hurt every time I said her name, a sharp stab in my heart. "Why would you be the exception?"

Her eyes flickered with doubt.

"Because I love her," Felix said fiercely, his grip around her waist tightening. "I've loved her ever since she was chosen by Neptune at the Stone of Destiny. So fierce, so strong. A beautiful goddess. We may not have long together, but once I'm in Elysium and she's won the Games, I'll be honored to have had her love, even if it was only for a short while."

Octavia smiled, apparently placated by his response.

"Pretty words from a pretty boy." Julian's voice was hard as stone.

"But not as pretty as when you promised Cassia an eternity with her in Elysium," I chimed in. "He didn't offer you that, did he?" I asked Octavia.

"Of course not," she said. "He believes in me. He knows I can win the Games. Unlike that stupid little bird, Cassia. She never stood a chance."

"So how will it feel," I started, tilting my head playfully. "If you win the Games and live your immortal life here, knowing that Felix is in Elysium laughing with Cassia about how easily he deceived you? How happy he'll be to never have to see you again?"

"He wouldn't," she said, although she pulled away from him slightly.

"Oh, he would." It was impossible to deny that I was having fun with this. "I've seen him with Cassia, and now, I've seen him with you. He looks at you with lust. But he looked at her with *love*."

"Stop this nonsense." Felix stood up, pushing Octavia down into the chair.

She looked startled for a second, but it was quickly replaced with anger. Anger toward me, anger toward Felix, or anger toward Cassia—I didn't know.

All I knew was that I was getting to her, and I was loving every moment of it.

"Everything I've done in these Games has been for *her*." He pointed to Octavia. "We've been an amazing team. You remember Antonia's reign as Empress of the Villa, right?"

"How could we forget?" Julian stiffened next to me. I had a feeling it was taking all his self-control not to break Felix's neck and rip his head off his body.

"Guess who was the brains behind that?" Felix squared his shoulders, continuing before we had a chance to reply. "Me."

I stared at him, unsure if he was joking or not.

Once it was clear that he wasn't, I laughed.

"Octavia went to that arena that week," I reminded him. "If you were the supposed mastermind of that week, then you *sent the person you claim to love* to the arena. That makes no sense."

"I volunteered to go to the arena." Octavia stood up, her murderous gaze fixated on me. "I wanted to kill Cassia. And I told Felix exactly how I intended to do it. Slowly and painfully. It turned him on just hearing about it." She looked to him and batted her eyelashes. "Didn't it, love?"

"You know it did." He marched over to Octavia, took her in his arms, and kissed her. Tongue and all.

I clenched my hands into fists.

Don't kill her now, don't kill her now, I thought, tempering the rage swelling inside of me.

There was bravery, and then there was stupidity. I hadn't got this far in the Games just to be murdered by the gods for breaking the rules. I refused to do that to myself, and I refused to do that to Julian.

Julian took my hand and squeezed it, as if he was thinking the same exact thing.

Eventually, Felix and Octavia broke apart to get some air. Felix's fingers were tangled in her hair, and he pulled at it roughly, like a promise for later.

Octavia was still pressed against him, breathless. She was butter in his hands.

It didn't take long for her to compose herself and face

us again. "It wasn't easy to get time alone with Antonia before the selection ceremony, but I managed," she said. "I told her what I'd heard in the sauna—about how Felix was also with Cassia. I told her I was coming to her as a friend. She didn't believe me—at least not fully. She truly thought Felix wanted her. He had her wrapped around his finger."

"Sounds like he had her wrapped around something else," Julian muttered, glancing at Felix's breeches.

I bit down on my cheek to stop myself from chuckling. None of this was funny, but at the same time, it was so dark and twisted that I was constantly on the brink of snapping.

Angry whirlpools swirled in Octavia's ocean blue eyes. "We had to make Cassia Antonia's target," she said, each word sharp and measured. "That little seed of doubt was enough. But there was still one final part of the equation."

"Pierce," I realized.

"He could have turned on you," Julian said. "He was considering it."

"He wasn't," she said smugly. "The two of you were so focused on each other that you missed something huge right in front of you."

"And what was that?" I asked.

"Emmet and Pierce," she said. "They were far more than just friends."

My lips parted. Because the early morning workouts they did together, their time in the bathhouse afterward… it clicked instantly.

"They were lovers," I said.

"That they were." Octavia smiled.

Julian cursed. Apparently he hadn't realized it, either.

"So you figured it out, and promised him you wouldn't tell anyone else if he teamed up with you in the arena," I guessed.

"I could have." She smirked. "But I did something even better."

Felix lowered his lips to her neck and smothered her with small kisses. "My beautiful warrior is so conniving," he said, and she sighed from his touch.

My stomach twisted in disgust.

"Tell me, Octavia," I said, since she loved gloating nearly as much as she loved Felix's kisses. "What did you offer Pierce?"

She shrugged Felix off, but he kept his arm wrapped around her waist. From the glint in her eyes, I could tell she liked controlling him. "I offered to do what he couldn't," she said. "I promised him that when the time came, I'd be the one to take Emmet out. And that I'd do it quickly and painlessly."

"You didn't stick to your word," I said, recalling how she'd carved her name all over Emmet's skin until he passed out from blood loss. She'd waited until he was unconscious to shoot an icicle through his heart.

"I didn't have to." She shrugged. "Pierce was already dead."

"Would you have kept your word if he hadn't been?" Julian asked.

She took a second to think about it. "Probably," she decided. "It wouldn't have been any fun, but it would have kept Pierce from turning against me."

"I'm surprised you didn't jump into bed with Pierce and Emmet, too," I said to Felix.

"I'm not attracted to men." He shrugged. "Although I would have done it, if it was necessary to protect myself and Octavia. Just like sleeping with Cassia was necessary. I hated every moment that I had to pretend to be in love with her, but I did what I had to do. For Octavia."

"Not for Octavia," I corrected him. "For yourself." I turned to Octavia, ready to drop what I hoped would be a major blow. "You weren't the only person to volunteer to go to the arena," I said. "Because Felix volunteered, too."

SELENA

"WHAT?" Felix looked at me like I was crazy. "I'd never volunteer for the arena."

"Lies." My electricity crackled and popped, sparks of it landing on the rug near my feet.

"I'd never do anything that stupid," he said.

"You're the liar," I said to him, refocusing on Octavia. "It was how he made the final four deal with me, Julian, and Cassia on the second week, when you were Empress of the Villa. He promised that if Julian, Cassia, or I won Emperor of the Villa, he'd go to the arena with you and Cillian so Cillian could take you out. It was his idea."

"You seriously expect her to believe that I'd volunteer to be in the arena with a madman?" Felix asked. "He could have killed me! He would have killed me, if he'd managed to get out of those vines."

"Wrong," Julian said. "Octavia wouldn't have fought you. She would have attacked Cillian. Cillian would have defended himself, and killed Octavia."

"Those were your exact words," I said. "When you offered us the deal."

Felix's eyes narrowed. "Your lies don't even make sense."

"They're not lies," I said.

"Of course they are!" he said. "If I wanted Cillian to take out Octavia, I would have told him how to escape the vines. But I didn't. Because I *wanted* Octavia to kill him."

"You didn't because it wasn't part of our deal!" Julian slammed his fist into the end table next to him, splintering it to pieces. "You couldn't give away that you were working with us."

"Because *I wasn't working with you.*" Felix's face turned bright red. "And I never volunteered to go to the arena!"

"YES, YOU DID." Julian hurled himself at Felix. But he stopped at the marble game table, picked it up, and smashed it to the floor.

The pieces of marble flew into the air, and I had to move to the side to stop one from hitting me.

There was a deep dent in the floor where he'd thrown it.

I hurried to Julian and placed my hand on his forearm. He was so angry that I could feel the blood throbbing through his veins.

"Felix is lying," I said to Octavia. "And you're too blinded by him to see it."

"*You're* lying," Felix said with so much conviction that I wondered if he actually believed it.

He repulsed me so much that I couldn't even look at him.

"You're just going to stand there and say nothing?" I goaded Octavia. "He's lying. If you're as close to him as you claim, you have to know it."

Octavia remained perfectly still as she sized up Julian and me.

Then, she cozied closer to Felix.

"Felix would never volunteer to go to the arena," she said. "He knows his strengths and weaknesses. He wouldn't risk himself like that."

"He would," I said. "And he *did*."

"Lies." Felix let go of Octavia and threw his hands in the air. "Lies, lies, lies. All of it is *lies*! I know it, Octavia knows it, and the entire Otherworld knows it."

I shot a bolt of lightning inches away from Felix's feet. He jumped straight into Octavia's arms.

Weakling.

"You knew Felix could get out of those vines," I said to Octavia, since Felix wasn't worth the effort. "You had to have seen it. So why didn't he free himself? Why didn't he help you fight Cillian?"

"Because I didn't need the help." She smirked. "If he'd dropped, I would have had to worry about keeping *both* of us safe from those wild beasts while I was taking out Cillian. His dropping would have only been a hindrance. By staying up there, he was helping me."

"Because he's weak." I scoffed. "I'm surprised, Octavia. For someone so strong, I'd think you'd want someone better than a twerp like him."

Crystals of ice spread from her palms and up to her elbows. "Felix might not excel in the arena," she said with a twisted grin. "But trust me—he excels in places far more important." She reached down and stroked the inside of Felix's thigh.

He shuddered in pleasure, like he wanted to take her then and there.

"He also excels in lying." Julian's eyes were locked on Felix's.

"You're the one who's lying!" Felix said, pulling away from Octavia's touch. "You're grasping at straws, saying things that don't even make sense!"

"You wanted Cillian to kill Octavia," I said darkly. "And when he didn't, you scurried over to her like the rat you are."

"I couldn't have scurried over to her, because I've been with her since the beginning!"

I let go of Julian's arm and shot another bolt of lightning near Felix's feet. "Just admit it!" I shot another bolt, and then another, so he was cowering in Octavia's arms. She didn't even flinch. "You're using her. Just like you were using Cassia. Just like you use *everyone*."

I went to shoot another bolt, but Julian reached for my arm, stopping me. "Selena," he warned. "Don't."

I nearly flung him off of me.

Instead, I called my magic back inward. Because Julian was right.

We needed to get out of there before either of us did something we'd regret.

Felix relaxed and smiled smugly. "We played the two of you, and we played Cassia," he said. "Get over yourselves and just admit it."

"You're a slimy piece of shit," Julian raged. "I can't wait to kill you." His skin heated. Every muscle in his body was taut.

"He's not going to budge." I urged Julian toward the doors. "Let's go."

Julian stayed put and clenched his fists tighter. "The entire Otherworld's laughing at you, Octavia," he said to her. "You won't win the Games. But I hope you can watch the recordings in Elysium, so you can see how badly you were played."

He gave Felix one final fiery look, spun around, pulled me out of the room, and practically dragged me up with him to the suite.

33

SELENA

THE MOMENT I closed the door to the suite, Julian picked me up, pressed me up against the wall, and kissed me.

This kiss was hungry. Hot. Intense. And I didn't even care that the orbs were watching us, broadcasting us to everyone in the Otherworld.

Let them watch us.

Let them know exactly what they were destroying by pitting Julian and I against each other in the Games.

I wrapped my legs around his waist and kissed him back with pure, raw passion, until the entire fight from downstairs was gone from my mind. All I could think about was Julian. His strong arms around me, the heat of his skin, the taunting pressure of his hips moving against mine.

He spun around, his hands under my thighs as he

carried me to the bed and threw me down onto it. He lowered himself until there was only an inch of torturous space between us. His eyes burned with need, and desire, and maybe even with love.

I love you. The words were on my lips, aching to come out.

Instead I stared at him, breathless, my heart pounding so loudly that he must have been able to hear it.

He kissed me again, his tongue probing against mine. The hardness in his breeches brushed against my leg, and his hand caressed the inside of my thighs, teasing me with the promise of more.

I wrapped my arms around his neck and pulled him closer. "Julian," I begged, my back arching up to close the space between us. "Please."

Finally, when I didn't think I could take it for a second longer, he slipped his fingers inside of me and gave me the release I so desperately needed.

I wanted more. But I also wanted him to lose himself in me like I'd just lost myself in him. So I reached into his breeches, my fingers lingering over his birthmark that matched mine before I moved downward and took his hardness in my palm. As he rocked against me, he moaned and said my name over and over, his cries getting more and more desperate until he came apart in my hand.

We wrangled ourselves fully out of our clothing, smothering each other with kisses as we crawled our way under the covers. His skin was hot against mine, and he held me against him, snuggling me into a cocoon of warmth. I'd never felt as safe as I did in Julian's arms. I may not have been home in Avalon, but I'd found a different type of home, here with Julian.

I closed my eyes, promising myself to always remember this moment.

"Selena," he murmured into my hair. "I love you. You know that, right?"

I pulled back to gaze into his beautiful ice blue eyes. They were open and vulnerable. His soul was mine. I wasn't sure what I'd done to deserve something so pure and perfect, but I was going to appreciate every single second of it.

"I love you, too." A weight lifted off my shoulders after saying the words I'd known were true for longer than I cared to admit. "You're the only one I've ever loved. The only one I *will* ever love."

He smiled—pure, radiant happiness. "You're the only one I've ever loved, too."

I bit my lip and glanced down, only for a second.

That second was all he needed to reach for my chin and raise my eyes to meet his again.

"What's wrong?" he asked, his voice brimming with concern.

"Nothing," I said, heat rushing to my cheeks. "It's nothing."

He watched me, waiting. He knew it wasn't true. He wasn't going to force it out of me, but at the same time, I wanted to ask. I *needed* to ask. Because now that I knew he loved me, and he knew I loved him, there was only one thing holding me back from being with him completely.

"You said I'm the only one you've ever loved," I started, anxiety building inside me with each word I spoke. "But what about the princess who nominated you for the Games? Princess Ciera?"

"You saw that," he muttered. "Of course you saw that."

I nodded, but he was barely looking at me, refusing to meet my eyes.

"It was before we knew each other," I said, each word coming faster. "And she's beautiful. I understand why you'd..." I trailed off, unable to say that he wanted her. "I saw the way she looked at you. And I just wanted..." My cheeks heated again, and I cursed myself for bringing it up at all.

"Selena," he said my name, steady and true. And as I stared up at him, I realized that no matter who he'd been with in the past, his heart had always been mine, just like mine had always been his. "You're my soulmate. We were literally made for each other. I love you. And I'll always be honest with you. So yes, Princess Ciera and I were intimate with each other. But nothing more than what the two of us have done together so far. I told her that..." He lowered his eyes in shame, the same way he'd looked after bringing me to the Otherworld.

"It's okay," I said softly, tracing my finger along his cheekbone. He closed his eyes, relishing in my touch. "Whatever it was, it's okay."

"But it's not." He opened his eyes and focused on me once more. "She wanted me, and I went along with it, since only princes and princesses can nominate half-bloods for the Games. She was my ticket in."

"But that doesn't make sense," I said. "If she cared for you, why would she put you in so much danger?"

"Because I was a half-blood, and she was a princess," he said. "I told her I wouldn't fully give myself to her until I was her equal. And the only way to become her equal was for her to nominate me for the Games, for me to get chosen, and for me to win."

"And after you won?" I didn't know why I'd asked, when I wasn't sure I wanted to know the answer.

"After I won, I'd be able to give my family security for the rest of their lives," he said. "That was all I cared about. Princess Ciera gave me the chance to do that for them, so I took it. But by nominating me for the Games, she also gave me a chance to get to know you—to learn that we're soulmates. It wasn't the most noble way to get here, and I'm not proud to admit it. But I wouldn't change a thing. Because in the end, it brought me to you. I love you, Selena. And if all we have is this final night together—"

"Don't talk like that," I interrupted. "We have a plan. It's going to work. You believe that, right?"

"I hope it works," he said. "But if it doesn't, I'll fight the gods before ever laying a hand on you."

His eyes were so fierce—burning with all the intensity of the chosen champion of Mars—that I knew it was true. But tonight, I didn't only want the chosen champion of Mars. I wanted Julian. All of him.

I wrapped my leg around his waist and kissed him, our hearts beating in time together. "I love you," I said between kisses, my heart swelling each time he said the same. These kisses were softer than the ones before—gentle and full of love.

He rolled on top of me, his body hovering above mine as he looked down at me in question.

I nodded, and he smiled as he lowered his lips to kiss

me again, threading his fingers through my hair as he slid himself inside of me.

I gasped, and he paused to make sure I was okay.

"Yes," I said breathlessly, pushing my hips up so he could fill me completely.

We moved perfectly in time together, losing ourselves in each touch, each movement, each time we said we loved each other. Every nerve in my body lit on fire. Desire built in my core, until I was on the edge of exploding from the ecstasy inside of me.

And when I did—when we both did—I knew down to my soul that my love for Julian was everlasting, from this world and into the Beyond.

34

TORRENCE

"THREE WEEKS," I said to Sage once she came to my room to get ready for breakfast. "That's how much time has passed for Selena since we got to this island. And in our three days here, we've done *nothing*."

"We figured out that Circe can't hear through the sound barrier you put around your room." She looked around at the walls that were gilded with gold—and infused with my magic. "So at least we can speak freely. It's a start."

I stood up and started pacing around. I'd been doing a lot of that in the time that we'd been there. "We should have already killed her, gotten the staff, and been out of here," I said. "And if she touches me one more time…" I wrapped my arms around myself and shuddered at the thought of Circe's advances.

It was only a slight brush of the fingers here and there, and sitting closer to me than was comfortable. But it was happening more and more each day. Not just to me, but to Sage, too—although Sage was much better than I was at playing her part and flirting back.

Each time Circe set her predatory gaze on me, it felt like she was undressing me with her eyes. From the way she smiled at me—like I was a challenge meant to be conquered—I assumed she was taking her time because she had a year to toy with me. And she was enjoying every single second of it.

The only thing that stopped me from snapping at her and slapping her hands away was thinking of Selena.

Sage and I had the best chance of getting the staff if neither of us were turned into pigs. And I wouldn't fail my best friend by losing control of my emotions and making a move against Circe.

At least, that was what I kept telling myself.

But I wasn't sure I'd be able to keep reining it in if—no, *when*—Circe pushed further.

"She won't touch you anymore." Sage came up to me and took my hands in hers, stopping my pacing. Her eyes were hard—resolved. "Because I'm going to move forward with the first plan Thomas proposed to Reed."

I dropped her hands and stepped back. "No." I looked

to the door, and then back to Sage. "You can't do that. What about Thomas?"

"Thomas will be stuck as a pig forever if we don't use whatever means necessary to get the staff."

"But he's your mate," I said. "You can't do that to him."

"I can, and I will." She stood strong and held my gaze —a true alpha wolf. "Unless you want to do it?"

I held my breath and pressed my lips together. I *should* have said yes. Anything for Selena.

But I knew what I'd be committing myself to if I did. And the thought of letting Circe kiss me, undress me, and do whatever else she wanted to do to me... would I truly be able to convince her that I was enjoying it?

No, the answer came to me, even though I wished I could say otherwise. *You wouldn't.*

"I'm going to spend the day with her and shower her with the attention she desires," Sage continued, apparently having gathered my answer from my silence. "Tonight, I'll go with her to her bed. Once she's asleep, I'll kill her and steal the staff." Her hands shifted into claws, her teeth sharpening into points. Then she shifted them back. "She might have taken our weapons, but I *am* a weapon. I can do this."

"You shouldn't have to," I said. "There has to be another way."

Sage sat on the chair in front of my vanity and grabbed a tube of lipstick. "This will be the fastest." She applied it and looked back at me. Her lips were as bright red as Circe's—the color of a true enchantress. "Unless you have a better idea?"

I didn't.

But I couldn't let her do this.

I started pacing again. I needed to think, and *quickly*.

So far, our plan had consisted of tracking Circe's routine to figure out the best time to attack. But Sage was right. The only time Circe let her guard down was when she was sleeping. And she'd spelled her bedroom so we couldn't enter uninvited. She'd told us that on the tour she'd given us on the first day.

Even if we could enter uninvited, Circe was sharp and quick. She'd shown that when she'd turned the guys into pigs. She'd know the moment we turned the door-knob, and then we'd likely be enjoying time in the sand with Thomas, Reed, and all the other pigs on that beach.

As much as I didn't want to admit it, Sage was right.

The only way to be close enough to attack Circe unaware was to go to bed with her and be right next to her while she was sleeping.

Unless…

Were we going about this all wrong? Could we get the staff *without* attacking her?

A crazy idea hit me, and I stopped pacing.

"What?" Sage asked.

While I'd been thinking, she'd painted on winged eyeliner, pulled down the neckline of her top, and applied contour on her cleavage to make her breasts appear larger.

Ugh. I hoped she'd be on board with my idea. Because while it might be out there, it was better than what she was intending to do with that *witch*.

And I meant that in the meanest sense of the word. Which I was allowed to do, since I was one.

I sat down on the foot of the bed and placed my hands on my knees. "Maybe we don't have to steal the staff," I said slowly.

"Yeah. We do." Sage looked at me like I'd been drugged with one of Circe's potions. "At least, we need to steal it if we want to get off this island within the next year and have a chance of getting to the Otherworld to save Selena."

"That's not what I meant," I said.

"Then what *did* you mean?" she asked. "Because I'm clearly having trouble following."

"Why do we have to attack Circe at all?" The words came faster as the idea continued formulating in my mind. "Why can't we just *ask* for the staff?"

Sage was silent. And not in a good way. It was the

type of silence where she was waiting for me to drop a punch line and say I was kidding.

Except there was no punch line.

"Because Circe won't just give us her staff," Sage said, speaking to me like I was a child.

"Why not?" I asked.

"Because it's her staff. She's had it for thousands of years."

"But she has potions that turn people into pigs," I said. "She doesn't need the staff to do that. And Avalon has tons of resources. The Earth Angel will give anything to get Selena back."

"Except for the Holy Grail and Excalibur," Sage said.

"Are you so sure about that?"

"No." Her eyes hardened. "But those are the holy items from the prophecy. We need them to defeat the demons. We can't ask the Earth Angel to trade them."

"We can't?" I challenged. "Or *you* won't?"

"I won't," she said. "And neither will you."

"There has to be something she wants in exchange," I said. "Avalon has lots of valuable items hidden in the basement vaults."

Her eyes narrowed. "How do you know about the vaults?" she asked.

"My best friend is the Earth Angel's daughter." I shrugged. "I know things."

Sage rested her elbows back on the vanity and studied me. "Let's say we do this," she said. "What's to stop Circe from saying we're crazy and turning us into pigs on the spot?"

"Nothing," I said. "But she'll definitely turn us into pigs if we attack and fail. If we're honest with her, maybe she'll listen."

Sage said nothing.

"And how confident are you that you'll be able to go through with your plan for tonight?" I continued. "Thomas is your *mate*. You love him, and he loves you. I've seen the way you look at each other. Do you truly think you'll be able to do this tonight? And would you be able to live with yourself if you do?"

More silence.

Then, Sage reached for a cloth and wiped the red from her lips. "Fine," she said once all the lipstick was gone. "We'll try this your way. And if it doesn't work… at least Circe will stop trying to seduce us if we're pigs. At least, I *think* she will."

35

TORRENCE

SAGE and I told Circe everything at breakfast, starting with Selena's kidnapping. From the way she sipped her tea and listened without many interruptions, she at least seemed interested.

I breathed easier once we finished telling her the entire story without her lashing out and turning us into pigs.

"We have many precious objects in the Avalon vaults to trade with," Sage said. "We keep them protected there, safe from anyone who might try to steal them, saving them for a time in the future when they'll be absolutely necessary."

"Very sensible." Circe nodded. "What objects do you have?"

I looked at Sage, since while I knew there were

important objects in the vaults, I didn't know exactly what they were.

"Armor that will always protect you from physical injuries," she said. "A shield that grants its owner heavenly protection. A bow that will never miss its mark. A dagger that will shroud its user in shadow. A sword that will only kill those who deserve it."

"That's it?" Circe asked.

"They're all highly valuable," Sage said. "They were left for us on Avalon by King Arthur."

"They might be valuable to you." Circe's grip around her staff tightened. "But they have no value for me. Plus, I'd never trade my staff. It was foolish of you to think I would."

"Please," I begged. "There must be something you want."

She smiled, slow and seductive. "There *is* something I want," she said. "The two of you on my island for the rest of the year. Therefore, I already have what I want. And while your story is compelling, it's not my problem."

This was getting us nowhere. But there *had* to be something that would tempt Circe. There was always a way out of every situation. I just needed to figure out what that way was.

"What if you loan us the staff?" I asked. "Once we're

back from the Otherworld, the forces of Avalon can get it back from King Devin and return it to you."

"You'll be highly compensated for your cooperation," Sage added before Circe could respond.

Circe crossed her legs as she looked back and forth between us. "You're making many promises on behalf of your kingdom," she said. "Especially given that neither of you have any real power there."

"Our mission is to do everything necessary to get Selena home safely," Sage said. "The Earth Angel will honor any deals we make to succeed in this task."

She looked surprisingly confident, given that she was making this up. Sure, it was *likely* that the Earth Angel would do her best to follow through on whatever deals we needed to make to get Selena home. But she'd never said so explicitly.

"I'm not interested in making any deals with Avalon, or with your Earth Angel," Circe finally said. "I am, however, open to a deal with you." She looked at me when she said the final part.

Shivers spread from the top of my spine all the way down to my toes. "What did you have in mind?" I held onto the edges of my chair, bracing myself for whatever was coming next.

You don't have to agree, I reminded myself. *If she asks for too much, you can say no.*

And then blame myself if Selena ended up stuck in the Otherworld forever?

If that happened, I wouldn't be able to live with the guilt. And I was close to positive that Circe knew that, too.

"I'll loan you my staff for three months," she said. "If it's not back by the end of those three months, you'll come back to Aeaea and live here with me."

"For how long?" I asked.

"For forever."

I sat there, shell-shocked.

"Similarly to how you described life on Avalon, you'll be immortal on Aeaea, forever preserved as you are now," Circe continued. "No matter where you are—even if you don't survive your journey and you end up in the Underworld—you'll be instantly transported to Aeaea if three months pass and I still don't have my staff. The deal will ensure it."

She watched me, waiting. But my tongue felt numb.

She can't ask this of me.

Except she could. And she had.

"Don't take Torrence." Sage reached for Circe's free hand and gripped it in hers. "Take me instead."

"You're married. You've been tarnished." Circe sneered, yanking her hand out of Sage's, and refocusing on me. Her eyes softened. "You, my dear, are untouched and pure. You're the one I want. So tell me… how badly do you want to save your friend?"

I pressed my lips together. Because she knew the answer to that.

She was just toying with me now. And I refused to let her get away with it.

"Immediately after the deal is sealed, you promise to turn Thomas and Reed back to normal, loan us the staff, and let the four of us leave the island on our yacht without forcing us to return?"

I'd learned enough about deals to know that the exact wording was always important.

"Yes." She smiled. "Except for you, of course, if you fail to return my staff. I promise."

"Okay. I'll do it," I said before I could stop myself.

"No." Sage looked at me in horror. "There has to be another way."

"There isn't." I placed my palms flat on the table, steadying myself. "And even if there is, we don't have the time to figure out how. *Selena* doesn't have the time for us to figure it out. I'm doing this for her. This is our best chance, and you know it."

Sage's eyes burned with intensity. "We'll get that staff back in three months," she said, turning to Circe. "I'll make sure of it."

"Very well." Circe raised an eyebrow, pushed out of

her chair, and stood up. "Torrence," she said. "Come stand in front of me."

I did as she asked, facing her with my head held high.

"Sealing the deal is easy." She raised the hand that wasn't holding the staff and traced her finger along my cheek. "It only takes one kiss."

I held her eyes, staying as still as a statue. A kiss might be the way to seal the deal, but I'd make sure she knew I didn't enjoy it.

She moved closer and pressed her lips to mine. They were ice cold and tasted like bitter poison. A chill swept through my body, growing colder and colder until I feared I might be turning to ice. I tried pulling away, but I was frozen in place. Powerless.

Panic raced through my chest.

She'd deceived us. She was killing me.

Sage, I thought, although I couldn't move my head to look at her. *Do something. Stop her. Please.*

I wasn't breathing. Everything around me turned into a milky haze. My heart beat slower, and slower. Soon, it would stop altogether.

This was it. This was how I was going to die.

But then, Circe pulled away.

Warmth flooded through me. My heart picked up speed until it was beating normally. I could breathe.

I flexed my fingers, surprised at how easily they moved.

"That wasn't so hard." Circe tilted her head, her eyes dancing as she looked at me. "Was it?"

"No." I forced a smile. "It wasn't."

The corner of her red lips curled up in amusement. She reached for a strand of my hair and started to pull it over my shoulder, but I slapped her hand away.

"Showing your true colors." She dropped her arm to her side. "I like it."

Sage was immediately by my side, her fingers shifted into claws. "Bring us to Thomas and Reed, change them back, and send us off," she said, her true alpha self shining through as she stared Circe down.

"Of course." Circe held her staff in front of her with both hands, warding Sage off. "I'm a woman of my word. And while I'd usually wish you luck, there's no need to bother with the pleasantries. Because you both know I'm hoping you'll fail."

She gave me another seductive smile, turned on her heel, and led us out to the beach.

36

TORRENCE

SAGE, Thomas, Reed, and I stood on the top deck of the yacht as we sailed off. I held onto the staff, feeling its power pulse through me.

Circe stood on the beach, her dress and hair blowing in the wind. She blew me a seductive kiss and winked.

I didn't move my gaze from hers. *Three months*, I thought, my grip tightening around the staff. *I'll be returning this to you in less than three months.*

"From the way she's looking at you, I'd say you bewitched her," Reed said with a scowl.

I yanked my gaze away from Circe's and focused on him. Everything about him was calm, except for his eyes. They raged with emotion.

"What if I did?" I asked, swallowing down disgust at the knowledge of what I'd *actually* done.

"Then you're no better than the sluts at the Tower."

I flinched backward, a storm brewing inside me. "I think you're forgetting that if it wasn't for me and Sage, you'd be stuck on that island as a pig for the rest of eternity."

"We would have figured out a way to shift back," he said.

I rolled my eyes at his arrogance. "You really can't just say thank you," I said. "Can you?"

"You went to Circe's bed to get her staff." He looked at me, repulsed. "I expected better from you."

I slammed the end of the staff into the floor. "I did what I had to do to get the staff," I said. "Which is far more than I can say for you."

He held my gaze, glaring at me. "You should have kept that dress they gave you at the Tower," he finally said. "Apparently, it suited you."

Thomas was beside us in an instant. "Enough," he said, looking back and forth between Reed and me. "You," he said to Reed. "Stop making assumptions."

I stood taller, smirking at Reed.

"And you," Thomas said to me. "Stop goading him. It's not getting us anywhere."

"I'm not—"

"You are," he said. "Now, would you care to share exactly how you got Circe to hand over her staff?"

The reality of what I'd done crashed over me again. It was a good thing I was holding onto the staff, because I needed something to keep me balanced.

There was no way I was getting away with what I'd done without any repercussions. I knew it deep in my soul.

Sage moved to my other side and placed her hand gently on my arm. "Let's go downstairs," she said. "Because it's a lot to take in, and I think all four of us should sit down while we explain."

Thomas stored the staff in the closet with the girdle. Then the four of us sat around the table, and Sage and I shared what had happened after the two of them were turned into pigs.

"That was the deal Circe offered," I said, finishing up the story. "And I accepted."

Reed's eyes were stone cold. They'd been like that the entire time Sage and I shared what we'd done on Aeaea. "Turn the boat around," he said to Thomas. "We're giving Circe back the staff."

"No," I said. "We're not. At least, not until Selena's back home and we get the staff back from King Devin."

Thomas rested his elbows on the table and sighed.

"We might not get the staff back from King Devin," he said.

"Of course we will," I said. "Avalon has resources. We're allied with him. We'll find a way to get it back."

"Yes, we're allied with the Tower," he said. "And that alliance is more important to Avalon than you are."

His words were a punch in the gut. "I'm risking everything to help Selena," I said. "The prophetess chose me for this mission. Avalon will protect me in return."

"Selena is the Earth Angel's daughter," he said. "She was taken against her will. You entered into this agreement on your own. If you fail, you'll be expected to keep your word."

"We won't fail," Sage said.

"No, we won't." Reed stood up and headed for the steps. "Because we're giving that staff back to Circe. Right now."

"You can't control the yacht," Thomas said calmly. "It's under my control."

Reed raised his hand and blasted Thomas with his magic.

Thomas crashed into the wall behind him and crumpled to the floor.

Sage shifted and pounced on Reed, but he blasted her to the ground while she was mid-air.

"Stop!" I ran to Reed and gripped his wrists in my

hands. He glared at me, but he didn't use his magic against me. "What are you doing?"

"I'm doing what's necessary to get this boat back to that island so we can return that cursed staff."

We stood like that for a few seconds, locked in a standstill. His eyes were pools of ink, his skin ridiculously warm against mine. The memory of his kiss tingled on my lips as his magic called to me, tendrils of it licking my skin and begging me to let it in. A breeze blew around us. His magic was so raw, so powerful, so *alive*. If I let it, I knew it would consume me completely.

He would consume me completely.

So I envisioned a shield of my purple magic surrounding me, blocking his out.

"What do you care if I end up on Aeaea for all of eternity?" I searched his eyes for answers, but I found none. "You hate me."

He pulled out of my grip and stepped back. The air around us was still again. "You're one of the most impulsive people I've ever met, and I find you frustrating as hell," he said. "But you don't deserve to end up in that place for all eternity. No one does."

"Then help me get the staff back from King Devin before the three months are over."

Suddenly, Sage and Thomas zipped around to stand to our sides. Sage held Circe's staff, and the top of it was angled at Reed. "Use your magic against us again, and I'll turn you back into a pig," she said.

"You're telling me that you're okay with what she did?" He glanced at me, and then turned his attention back to Sage.

"It was my decision," I said. "I didn't need anyone's permission."

"It was a *stupid* decision," Reed said.

Thomas stepped forward and held both his hands out to stop Reed and me from fighting. "What's done is done," he said. "We have the staff, and all four of us made it off the island unscathed. We can't delay the mission further. We have to move on, and handle the repercussions of Torrence's decision when the time comes."

"King Devin is willing to trade the items we need to enter the Otherworld for the items he requested," I said. "Once our mission is complete, all we have to do is offer him another trade. Then we can get Circe's staff back to her before the three months are up."

"Your confidence is either courageous or naive," Reed said. "I'm not sure which one yet."

"I guess we'll find out in the next three months," I replied.

"I guess we will," he said. "Although if I hadn't gotten myself turned into a pig, you wouldn't have been in this position at all. So it's only right that I stay by your side until that staff is back in Circe's hands."

I stared at him in disbelief.

That was the *last* thing I'd expected him to say.

"Thanks," I finally said. "That's very thoughtful of you."

He simply nodded, and turned to Thomas. "I'm sorry for using my magic against you," he said, glancing at Sage as well. "Against *both* of you. It won't happen again."

Sage lowered the staff. "Thank you for the apology," she said.

"Yes," Thomas agreed. "Thank you." Then he turned to face me. "Your actions today were brave."

"I did what was necessary to help Selena."

"You did," he said. "And once she's safely home, I promise to do everything in my power to convince Avalon to give you whatever support they can in helping you return that staff."

I smiled, since I knew he'd help me. Everyone on Avalon would come through for me. They were my family.

"But for now, we need to stay focused on the mission," he said. "Because we still have two more objects to find, and after losing three days on that island, we need to find them quickly."

37

SELENA

THE DAY WAS HERE. The final Emperor of the Villa competition—and the final day of the Faerie Games. Because with only four of us left, whoever won this Emperor competition wouldn't have a choice to make about who they were sending to the arena.

Instead, the four of us would be brought straight to the Coliseum, where the Emperor of the Villa would watch the three others fight it out. Once the first of those three champions was out, the Emperor of the Villa would join the remaining two in the arena, and the three of them would battle it out until only one remained.

The winner of this year's Faerie Games.

As my private carriage flew toward the city, reality set in.

The Nephilim army isn't coming for me. And both Julian and I might not make it through this day alive.

The Nephilim army had been my clutch for the entire two months that I'd been in the Otherworld. They were the light that had kept me from descending into total darkness.

No, that wasn't true. I also had Julian.

I *have* Julian.

All wasn't lost until one or both of us were dead. And we had zero intentions of letting it get that far.

Maybe my belief that Julian and I could get through this together was foolish, just like my belief in the Nephilim army had been. But last night, when Julian and I had solidified our love, I'd felt invincible.

I refused to let this be the end for us.

At the thought of last night, electricity crackled and sparked inside of me, ready to unleash its full force on whatever challenge I was facing next. Because I was going to fight with every last bit of magic inside me to make sure Julian and I had a future—not in the Underworld, but in *this* world—together.

The carriage landed in an open, grassy field, in line with the other three. Julian's was on one side of mine, and Felix's on the other.

Our coachmen jumped off their seats at the front of the carriages. They untied the pegasi, jumped on their backs, and flew off.

I tried to open the carriage door, but it was sealed shut. I pushed my bodyweight into it a few times, but nothing happened. And judging by how Julian also couldn't get out —and he was the physically strongest of us all—none of us were escaping. At least not until the gods allowed it.

I sat back down on the seat and surveyed the surroundings. The grassy field looked the same as the rest of the Otherworld countryside outside of the city. No people were anywhere to be seen. The only signs of life were the golden orbs buzzing around the carriages. They had, of course, followed us there.

The field went on for about a hundred yards ahead, ending at a grouping of hills. A giant, gaping cave entrance was right in the center of the tall hill in the middle.

Nothing good could be inside there.

We only sat in the carriages for about a minute more before a cloud overhead turned purple, and Bacchus flew out of it. With no crowd cheering him on, he didn't waste time with the dramatics of flying his chariot around in circles. He simply landed on the ground in front of us and stepped down.

The door to my carriage flew open, and I got out to face him. The others did the same.

I caught Julian's eyes for a second. He gave me a reassuring nod before turning his attention back to Bacchus.

No matter what happened in this competition, Julian and I could get through it. We'd discussed all the possible ways it could play out last night.

The best-case scenario would be if Felix won the emperor competition. He'd have to send me, Julian, and Octavia to the arena. From there, Julian and I would team up to take Octavia out in the first round of the final fight. It would be easy to take down Felix afterward, which would put Julian and me in the final two.

If Octavia won, it would be Julian and me against Felix. We could easily take him down. Then we just had to take down Octavia, and again—it would be one of our best bets to the final two.

If either Julian or I won, it would be the other one of us against Octavia and Felix in the first round of the arena fight. That was the least desirable of all the options. Because then the two of them would gang up against one of us, which would lower the chance of both of us making it to the final two. And even though Felix wasn't much of a physical threat, we still wanted to keep the odds in our favor.

Therefore, our strategy for this final emperor competition was simple.

Throw it to either Felix or Octavia.

And once Julian and I were in the final two, we had to pray that the rest of our plan worked, and that we'd both stay alive to see another day.

38

SELENA

BACCHUS FACED THE CLOSEST ORB, adjusted his purple toga, and gave his trademark grin. "Welcome to the final day of the Faerie Games!" he said. "This Emperor of the Villa competition is the first of the three events to happen today. Unlike the previous Emperor of the Villa competitions, the outgoing Empress of the Villa is eligible to compete." He glanced at me, and then turned his attention back to the orb. "The winner of this competition will be safe for the first part of the final, two part fight in the arena. As always, the three other champions will fight until one of them is dead. But then, the Emperor of the Villa will immediately enter the arena, and the three finalists will fight until there's only one left standing—the winner of this year's Faerie Games!"

It was strange to hear his usual enthusiasm without a crowd behind him cheering. But he didn't let the lack of a crowd detract from his performance.

"The way to become the final Emperor of the Villa is simple," he continued. "You see that cave over there?" The orbs in front of the cave glowed brighter, buzzing around to get a full view of it. "The Minotaur waits inside of it. Yes, *that* Minotaur—we borrowed him from his labyrinth so he could be with us today."

Bacchus raised his scepter and shot his purple magic toward the cave. The entrance shimmered, and the ground vibrated with the steady beat of giant footsteps.

Out came one of the most frightening monsters I'd ever seen.

It was as tall as a house, with the head of a bull and the body of a hairy troll. And as if the two horns sticking out of its head weren't dangerous enough, one of its hands had fingernails as long and pointy as swords. The other wasn't a hand at all, but an ax that started where its wrist should have been.

It growled at us, curling up its lips to show us its sharp pointy teeth. I would have thought it wanted to slice us up and eat us if I didn't know it was spelled by the gods to keep us alive.

It took four more steps forward, but the chains attached to its feet pulled tight, keeping it from going any farther. We weren't given any weapons, meaning we were supposed to fight the Minotaur using only our magic. Although with Julian there, we'd still be able to use weapons if we wanted to, since he could pull them out of the ether.

"The Minotaur will remain in chains for the entirety of the competition," Bacchus told us. "It won't attack unless provoked. So the question is—who wants to win this competition the most?"

Not me, I thought, keeping my eyes focused on the monster.

Bacchus climbed back into his chariot. "We're about to find out," he said, and the jaguars lifted him off the ground until he was floating higher than the Minotaur's head. "Because the competition starts NOW!"

None of us moved.

I glanced over at Octavia.

She just stood there, her arms crossed, smiling smugly. "Go on," she said, tilting her head toward the Minotaur. The monster was patiently waiting. "Unless both of you are too scared to face me solo in the first round in the arena?"

"Of course we're not," Julian said. "It's just strategy."

"Or cowardice." She shrugged. "That's the last thing I expected from the chosen champions of Mars and

Jupiter. But hey, they can't pick winners every time, can they?"

"Goading us isn't going to work," I told her. "So you might as well stop trying."

Felix walked over to Octavia, took her hands, and looked down at her like she was the light of his life. "They're not going for it," he said. "But you're strong enough to fight them on your own. You can beat them in *both* rounds in the arena."

"I know." She stood on her tiptoes and pressed a soft, lingering kiss onto his lips.

"So help me win this competition." He spoke to her so sweetly that he was clearly lacing his words with magic. "Bring me with you to the final two. Then, your hand will be the one to send me to Elysium. Just like we've wanted."

It sounded like bullshit to me. Felix was playing his odds, just like the rest of us. Because if he and Octavia made it to the final two—which Julian and I would make sure didn't happen—he'd likely try to pull off a move commonly used by chosen champions of Venus.

He was hoping that Octavia was so in love with him that she'd be unable to take his life, and that she'd take her own instead.

Octavia didn't strike me as someone who'd do something so selfless.

But from the way she was staring lovingly up into his eyes, it seemed to be working.

Then she blinked and took a step back, like she needed to put distance between them to think clearly. "I know I'm strong," she said. "But I'll also do everything I can to get both of us to the final two. Which means making sure neither of us wins this competition."

She pulled back her fist and swung it at Felix's head.

Julian was over there in less than a second. He shoved Felix to the side, and Octavia's punch whizzed through the air, hitting nothing.

Felix rolled over, betrayal shining in his eyes as he looked up at Octavia. It didn't stop her from moving to try knocking him out again. But Julian was on her in a heartbeat. The two of them fought using only their bodies—no weapons, and no powers.

The hand-to-hand combat was only a dance. They weren't actually hurting each other. Because they both wanted the other to remain physically able to beat the Minotaur.

Felix scurried out of the way.

"Only one of us can win," Octavia said to me in between punches. "You won't be able to hurt Julian." He nearly knocked her to the side, but she avoided his fist just in time. She aimed for his chest, but he blocked her again.

Julian sideswiped her leg and knocked her flat on her back. Then he called a sword from the ether and tossed it to me.

I easily caught it by the handle.

"Help Felix win," he said. "I'll keep the ice queen occupied."

Octavia stood up and blasted him with water. But he had a shield in front of him in a second, and he blocked her attack.

"Don't be stupid, Selena." Octavia snarled as she continued to try knocking Julian down with her water. But no matter how hard she pushed, he didn't break. "My magic is stronger than his. You know I can beat him."

"You're not doing a good job of it now," I pointed out.

She stopped blasting him with water and switched to icicles. He blocked them so easily with the shield that I suspected he could have read a book at the same time. "Only because I can't risk killing him," she said. "Win this competition. Send him to the arena with me and Felix, and let me do what you can't."

Julian ran at her, slashing through her icicles until he was close enough to slice off her hands. Instead, he flipped his sword around and jabbed the handle into her throat.

She fell back to the ground, her hands around her neck as she gasped for air.

Julian hovered over her, his sword held high. But he didn't take those final swings to eliminate her from the competition.

We needed to keep her in play in case Felix's attempt at taking down the Minotaur failed. And Julian was doing an excellent job keeping her controlled.

So I turned to Felix, who was standing hunched to the side as he watched all of this go down. His normal confidence was gone. All I saw was a meek little mouse.

"Do you want to win this competition?" I asked.

He glanced at where Julian and Octavia were fighting it out. Then he straightened and smirked, the meek mouse gone. "You bet I do."

"I thought as much." I walked forward and placed the sword on the grass between us. I didn't think he'd take a swing at me, but it was best to keep some space between us, just in case. "Take the sword. I'll go with you to the Minotaur to keep you protected. I'll fry it with my lightning, and once it's knocked out, you'll take the killing blow."

He picked up the sword and held it in front of him, getting used to its weight. "Sounds easy enough," he said, although his normal confidence was gone from his tone.

"The Minotaur will be knocked out." My electricity

sparked under my palms, but I held in my impatience. "You'll be fine."

He glanced over at the Minotaur. The monster was shifting its weight from one leg to the other, looking as ready to get this over with as I was.

"All right," he said. "Lead the way."

I glanced back at Julian and Octavia. The two of them were a blur as they continued exchanging blows.

Perfect.

Everything was going exactly as we'd wanted it to.

I gave Felix the go and headed toward the Minotaur. Felix followed at my heels.

The Minotaur perked up as we approached. It stepped forward again, pulling harder on the chains the closer we got. It was the biggest monster I'd ever faced.

Which meant I was going to have to throw a *lot* of lightning at it to knock it out.

Once I was as close to the monster as I could get while still staying out of its reach, I stopped and gathered my magic. It came to me easily, the electricity filling my body so it and I were one and the same. Spiderwebs of crackling light danced over my skin, begging to be released.

The orbs buzzed around me, and I smiled at them, even though I hated them.

One of them flashed dark for a second. A glitch,

maybe? I didn't think they could glitch, since they were created by the gods.

But it wasn't my problem. I had more important things to focus on. Like helping Felix kill this monster.

I looked away from the orbs, raised my hands, and hurled two bolts of lightning at the Minotaur's chest.

Its angry roar rang through the field. Its entire body lit up like a spotlight. I smelled the sharp, putrid scents of burning hair and skin. But it kept tugging at its chains, refusing to go down.

I kept the bolts locked on its chest, pushing my magic toward it. The light was so bright in front of my face that I could hardly see.

It roared again, followed by a loud snap from its direction. Another roar, another snap.

"Selena!" Felix cried out in warning.

I lowered my hands just in time to see the Minotaur's hand in front of me. One of its nails came at me to take my head off, but I dodged out of its path.

It shouldn't have been able to reach me. But a glance at its feet showed that it had broken free from the chains.

Then, a punch to the gut.

My breath caught, and I looked down.

One of its nails had gone straight through my stomach.

This couldn't be happening. But the electric light shining from my skin blinked once, twice, and then it went out.

The monster looked down at me, and something flashed in its eyes. Guilt, perhaps?

It pulled its nail slowly out of me. Sharp, twisting pain worse than I'd ever known ripped through me. I opened my mouth to scream, but nothing came out.

My hands went to my stomach, and I stumbled back, collapsing to the ground. Warm, sticky wetness flowed through my fingers.

Blood. So much blood.

If I was bleeding so much, why didn't it hurt?

My head lolled to the side. Felix had dropped his sword, and his mouth was open in shock.

My vision hazed around the edges. I tried to keep my eyes open, but the world continued to fade. So I pressed harder on my stomach to slow the blood. But I didn't even have the strength for that, and my hands dropped to my sides.

I couldn't move. Trying to think felt like wading through quicksand. All I could do was sink into oblivion.

Is this what it feels like to die?

A deep, guttural cry tore through my mind.

Julian.

His blurred form flew through the air, and then, everything went dark.

39

SELENA

I CRACKED MY EYES OPEN, and was assaulted by bright rays of light. I shut them quickly, and then opened them again, ready this time.

I was lying under the covers in bed. Julian sat next to me, his ice blue eyes shining with worry. The golden Emperor of the Villa wreath encircled his head.

Everything felt hazy and dreamy, like I wasn't really there. But Julian held my hand, and I squeezed tighter, grounding myself.

My stomach tingled with icy coldness.

The memory of the Minotaur slammed into me. All that blood... so much blood.

"Are we dead?" I asked Julian.

"No." He looked at me in wonder. "You're healed. We're both alive."

"Although you would have been dead," said a man with ink black curly hair sitting next to Julian. His skin was perfectly smooth, and his features were cut sharp. He had to be a supernatural of some sort. "If the Minotaur had its way."

"Who are you?" I pressed my other hand to my stomach. It was covered in a thick slab of salve.

"I'm Vejovis," he said. "The god of healing."

I sat up and recognized where we were—the healing chamber in the villa. I knew Vejovis healed us when we needed it, but I'd yet to meet the mysterious god.

"I usually leave my patients' sides before they wake," he continued. "But you required heavier monitoring, since you were nearly dead when I got to you. If Julian hadn't won the Emperor of the Villa competition when he did, you *would* have been dead."

I looked back to Julian, and the realization of what that wreath on his head meant sank in. "We needed to give that competition to Felix or Octavia," I said. "Why did you win it?"

"The Minotaur tried to *kill* you." His grip around my hand tightened, like he was afraid he was going to lose me at any second. "My back was toward the Minotaur when I was fighting Octavia. But then she stopped fighting, and I knew something had happened. I turned around, and there you were..." he trailed off, his eyes going distant before he refocused on me. "Bleeding out on the ground. You were dying, Selena. So I did the only thing I could do. I drove my sword through the Minotaur's heart and ended the competition."

"It's a good thing he did," Vejovis said. "Because once the competitions end, I'm allowed to come down and heal the champions who need it. By winning, Julian ended the competition and saved your life."

"I love you," I said to Julian, since it meant far more than any words of thanks.

I was starting to understand why the fae viewed a simple "thank you" as an inadequate expression of gratitude.

Vejovis looked back and forth between us. "We all saw Julian's birthmark when Minerva's chosen champion revealed it in the arena," he said. "I saw yours when I was healing you. There have never been soulmates in the Games before."

"This isn't new news," I said. "The orbs were around us when I told Julian that we're soulmates. That was after the *second* week of the Games. Surely the entire Otherworld knows by now."

"I'm bound by the spell not to reveal anything to either of you about this year's Games," he said. "But you may take my comment as you see fit."

Of course. Voicing simple factual statements was the

same way that Rufus—the half-blood who'd been in charge of me before I'd entered the arena the first time —had gotten around the spell.

"The gods must censor the live broadcasts," Julian said. "It's Bacchus, most likely, since he's in charge of the entertainment. And we've purposefully never mentioned that we're soulmates when anyone else is around."

"Except for Vesta and Venus," I reminded him.

"It seems they've been tight-lipped about it," he said. "Because apparently, no one else in the Otherworld knows we're soulmates."

"Which means…" I gave him a knowing look as the pieces fit together.

"Yes," he said. "Bacchus—or whoever's deciding what's shown to the fae—must have his reasons for keeping this from them. This may end up working in our favor even better than we planned."

"It may." Hope built in my chest at the possibility. But Vejovis couldn't know about what we had planned. No one could.

But maybe he had the answer to something else…

"The monsters aren't supposed to kill us in the emperor competitions," I said, changing the subject before Vejovis could ask Julian and I what we were talking about. "But the Minotaur tried to kill me."

"It did." Vejovis nodded. "It's very troubling."

"It wasn't the first to do so," I said. "The chimera tried to kill me, too." I gave Julian a meaningful look, since he, like the other champions, had thought I'd exaggerated when I'd said it after that competition.

"I should have believed you." His words gave me an immense amount of satisfaction. "I'm sorry."

"I understand why you questioned it," I said. "In the centuries since the Games have started, no monster has ever tried to kill a champion in an emperor competition. And no one else saw my fight with the chimera." Now, after learning that the broadcasts were censored, I wondered if anyone in the Otherworld had seen it, either. "It was far more likely that I was being paranoid than that I was right."

"But you're my soulmate," he said. "I never should have questioned you."

"Just don't do it again," I said with a smile.

"I won't," he said. "I promise." Then he turned his focus back to Vejovis. "This never should have happened," he said. "The gods must have plans to do something about it."

"What would you want them to do?" he asked. "All but one of you will die today." He turned his focus to me. "If you die, it matters not. If you live, you've earned your reward. Why complicate matters?"

"I've technically already been killed," I said, another plan forming in my mind. "Which should mean that I'm no longer in the Games."

"I can't believe I didn't think of that." Julian's eyes lit up. "We need to talk to Juno. Get her to—"

"If Juno was going to pardon you from the Games, she would have done so already," Vejovis interrupted. "The Olympians will not admit fault. Plus, they delight in watching the champions kill each *other* off. The only exception is if someone breaks the rules and gets themselves eliminated. They won't be satisfied with anything less."

"Apparently one of them would," I said. "Because that's the only way the spells on the monsters could have been broken, right? An Olympian had to have done it?"

"Diana is the goddess that puts the spells on the monsters," Vejovis said. "She's one of the most compassionate of the Olympians. She has no reason to want you dead."

That wasn't true.

"I sent her chosen champion to the arena the first week," I said. "I'm the reason that Molly's dead."

I never got to know Molly, and I deeply regretted it.

Just like I deeply regretted much of what I'd been forced to do during the Games.

I'd learned how to control my magic, but the power I

had at my fingertips had changed me. Early in the Games, I'd promised myself that I'd never delight in killing. But ever since watching Octavia torture and murder Cassia, I'd fantasized about how satisfying it would be when I finally got my vengeance and killed her.

I barely recognized who I'd become. And that scared me more than I cared to admit.

"Diana wouldn't blame you for Molly's death," Vejovis said. "The gods are well aware that the champions they choose likely won't make it out alive. Diana's champions rarely win, and she's never blamed the ones responsible for their deaths."

"Well, *someone* clearly wants me dead," I said.

"It's not Diana." Vejovis looked sure of it, and I believed him.

It was said that the gods chose champions who showed traits of themselves. Molly was sweet, and she didn't seem to have a violent bone in her body. Which meant Diana likely didn't, either.

"Maybe it's not Diana." Julian stared down Vejovis, as if that could force an answer out of him. "But there are eleven other Olympians. It has to be one of them."

I didn't know enough about the gods to guess which one it might be. And judging from their silence, Julian and Vejovis didn't, either.

"It could be one of the Olympians." Vejovis shrugged. "Or it could not. But like I said, the gods have been choosing champions for the Games for years. They've never broken any of the rules before. It seems unlikely they would now."

"But the Minotaur tried to kill me." I sat straighter, and frustrated sparks of electricity gathered in my palms. "Everybody saw."

Again, silence.

"I'm afraid I've stayed longer than I should." Vejovis stood, grabbed a damp washcloth from a nearby table, and used it to wipe the salve off my stomach. "Good as new," he said with a smile. "Now, I must take my leave. And I wish you both the best of luck in the final fight."

40

SELENA

I WASN'T GIVEN a skimpy gladiator costume to wear in the final fight to the death.

Instead, I wore a short dress similar to the one I wore for the Emperor of the Villa competitions. But this one was covered in sky blue jewels. I felt like a sparkly blue disco ball. Even the gold pointed tips on my ears were covered with sky blue gems. And my hair was down with soft curls in it, as was expected of the full-blood fae.

The message was clear.

Whoever won the final competition wouldn't emerge from the Games as a half-blood chosen champion.

They would emerge as an equal to the fae.

Julian had been pulled away from me right after

Vejovis had left the healing chamber. We didn't even get a chance to say goodbye.

But it wouldn't be the last time I saw him. I was going to make sure of it.

Now, I rode to the Coliseum in a carriage with Octavia and Felix. The two of them were so sickeningly snuggly the entire time. I hoped he'd shove his tongue so far down her throat that he'd gag her to death. Although then I wouldn't be able to kill her myself.

It was gross to watch, and it took all my effort not to shoot a lightning bolt between them to force them apart.

Instead, I stared out the window at the rolling countryside, mentally readying myself for the upcoming battle.

When the carriage dropped us off in the concrete halls beneath the arena, I was glad when Rufus helped me out. I couldn't hurry after him and away from the others fast enough.

We talked as we walked. I was glad to hear that his family was doing well. Plus, talking with him eased my nerves, just as it had the first time I'd entered the arena.

I couldn't believe that was only a few weeks ago. It felt like years.

Rufus led me to a glass box with a door cut into it, and he opened the door for me.

Please don't trap me inside of that thing, I thought, remembering how Cassia had nearly suffocated to death inside the igloo.

But the gods had already created a game that involved the risk of suffocating to death. If there was anything good I could say about the gods, it was that whichever one of them designed the games was creative. I doubted they'd do the same type of competition twice in one year.

I stopped in front of the box and took a deep breath. "You specifically requested me, didn't you?" I asked Rufus as I stepped inside.

"I'm not allowed to tell you who I favor in the Games." He looked at me with a spark of mischief in his eyes. "But don't you find it interesting that Jupiter's first ever chosen champion made it to the final four?"

"Yes." I shuffled my feet, my nerves firing with anticipation. "Quite."

"I have to close the door now," he said. "But your magic is stronger now. You know how to use it."

"I do," I said, already feeling the electricity thrumming inside of me. "And I plan on it."

He closed the door, and I pressed my palms against the glass wall of the box as it lifted up into the arena.

A path lined with hedges twice my height was in front of me. Beautiful pink, purple, and blue flowers bloomed from the bushes. The path came all the way around my box, locking the box inside.

An entrance to a maze.

Crap. I'd never been good at mazes. And I'd never attempted a life-sized one where I couldn't see the layout from above.

Feeling myself starting to panic, I looked up and over at the Royal Box. Sorcha sat regally in her throne. Julian sat in the throne beside her, the golden wreath on his head. He looked even more majestic than Sorcha. His eyes locked on mine, and I could practically feel the message he was sending me.

You can do this.

My electricity hummed louder. Because yes, I *could* do this. It wouldn't do me any good to believe otherwise.

In front of Julian and Sorcha—in the seats where the other champions normally sat—were four fae. Prince Devyn, Princess Ciera, and two others who I recognized as the fae who nominated Octavia and Felix for the Games. Each of them wore the color that represented the god who had chosen their nominee.

Maybe it was the confident way he was holding

himself, but Prince Devyn stood out more than the others in his sky blue robe. And he didn't look nervous in the slightest. Which made sense, since because of his gift, he knew the most likely way this competition would play out.

Princess Ciera kept preening herself and glancing back at Julian.

How can she be happy to see him?

But I quickly remembered that the gods hadn't broadcasted anything about me and Julian being soulmates.

That was going to be awkward with Princess Ciera later.

Assuming we *had* a later.

I looked around at the rest of the crowd. It was more packed than usual. Everyone held onto glasses of honey wine, sweetmeats, grapes infused with alcohol, cheeses, and other treats. The Coliseum had rained down more food and wine for this competition than any other.

Opposite the Royal Box was another box with five people in it. None of them had wings, they had red tattoos around their biceps, and they wore drab, unadorned clothing.

Half-bloods.

The three that stood out first were a man, a woman,

and a girl who looked to be their daughter. They had the same shiny, chestnut hair as Felix, and they were more striking than even the most beautiful full blooded fae. They had to be his family.

They were standing as far away as possible from the other two half-bloods. A thin woman with dark blond hair, her hands resting upon the shoulders of the frail, pale girl in front of her.

They had to be Julian's mother and his younger sister, Vita.

No one was there for Octavia.

Felix's mother glanced at Vita and moved closer to the other side of the box. She pulled her daughter along with her.

They must believe that Vita had the plague.

Idiots.

Bacchus's chariot hovered above the center of the arena. He raised his scepter, and the audience quieted. "As you can see, we took some inspiration from the Minotaur for the final showdown," he said. "A labyrinth! Except unlike a traditional labyrinth, once the champions enter this one, there will be no pathway out. The only way out is to be the last champion standing."

The crowd roared with delight and toasted with their wine.

"The biggest threats they'll face will be each other." Bacchus smiled down at us wickedly. "But that's all the information I feel like giving. They'll discover what else awaits them once they're inside. So now, let the first round of the final arena fight begin!"

41

SELENA

THE GLASS DOOR of my box opened unceremoniously.

The ground looked harmless, so I took a careful step out, holding my breath and waiting for something to happen. A bomb to explode, or some other surprise. But there was no bomb, and nothing burst from the dirt to wrap its tentacles around my ankles. There was only silence. I could no longer hear the crowd, and when I looked up, I saw only the sky.

It was just me and the maze.

Something tickled my back, and I jumped and spun around, coming face to face with vines that must have grown out of the hedges. The tips of the vines pushed against me, pricking my skin and nudging me forward.

While they didn't exactly hurt, they were irritating. So I did what they seemed to want and walked forward.

It didn't take long before I reached a point where the path branched into two directions. The annoying pricking of the vines ceased, and they pulled back.

I looked one way, and then the other. Right or left? They both looked the same.

I needed to see the layout of the maze from above.

So I picked a random side—left—and ran forward. Once I had enough momentum, I jumped.

My head smacked into something hard, and I crashed to the ground. Pain reverberated up my legs because I hadn't prepared myself for the fall.

What the hell? There definitely hadn't been anything in my way when I'd jumped.

But when I looked up, there was a thick branch sticking out of the hedge. The branch moved back into the bush—like it was growing backward in super speed —and disappeared.

I could try again and shoot lightning up to get past the branch. But that would alert the others to my location. It was too early to risk doing that. I needed to get my bearings, and figure out what I was up against in the maze.

So I ran back the way I came. This time when I jumped, I had my hand above my head, ready to incinerate any branch that came out to block me.

The branch shot out further down than where the

other one had, below my hand so it smacked into my forehead.

My butt crashed down onto the ground, and the world wobbled around me. I held my head in my hands for a few seconds to steady myself.

Trying to get a view from above wasn't working, and I was wasting time. So I walked back to where I'd started —the point where the original path broke into two. I looked right and left. Maybe I was missing something that would give me a clue about the direction I should go.

But both paths were identical.

Suddenly, something whooshed behind me. I spun around just in time to see the hedges closing up, blocking the path that led to my glass box.

Great. If I wasn't good with mazes to begin with, I definitely wouldn't be good at one where the paths changed.

Looked like this was going to be up to chance.

No, I realized. *Not chance.*

The gods had designed this maze so I'd cross paths with whoever they wanted me to find first.

Fine by me.

If it was Felix, it wouldn't be hard to defeat him. And if it was Octavia, I was ready to take her down.

"You can't control me." I looked straight into one of

the orbs buzzing around me, speaking softly to make sure the others wouldn't hear. "Only I can control my fate."

It was time to do just that.

I'd learned in one of the many television shows I'd watched on Avalon that if you were in a maze and always chose the path on the right, you'd eventually find your way out. Even though there was no path out of this maze, it seemed as good of a technique as any.

So I turned right, and then right again, and again.

I hit a dead end.

I started to turn around. But something moved out of the corner of my eye. I turned back around and saw a sword emerging from the hedge. It floated about a half foot forward and came to a stop.

The blade was made of sky blue crystal. A matching gemstone was encrusted in the handle.

The sword was beautiful. And it was made for me.

I walked forward to take it. But then I stopped and lowered my arms back to my sides.

Is this a trick? Will something terrible happen if I grab the sword? Something that pretty and tempting rarely comes without a price.

I hated this labyrinth.

But then my lightning sparked in my palms—a reminder that it was there. Despite my skill in sword fighting, swords hadn't helped me once in the Games. My magic was far more powerful than any other weapon I could yield.

The sword could have truly been made to help me. But was it worth risking it if it wasn't?

No. The answer came to me quickly. All the power I needed to win a fight was inside of me.

I backed away from the sword, my eyes locked on it with every step.

I don't need you.

I stepped out of the short path. The hedges on both sides of the entrance to the dead end grew inward, meeting in the middle and shutting completely.

I slowly moved my hand out to touch it, curious if the hedge would open again. Once I was about halfway through, thorns brushed against my palm. I yanked my hand back and examined it. The skin on my palm was fine, although from the sharpness of the thorns, I suspected it wouldn't have been if I'd pushed my hand through any quicker.

Don't fall into the bushes, I told myself. A ton of prickly thorns tearing through my skin might be more painful than a sword through the gut.

I continued forward, about to turn right at the next intersection. But something soft brushed around and between my ankles. I jumped back—making sure not to jump toward the hedges—and looked down.

A fluffy white cat with sharp topaz eyes sat down in front of me. It looked up at me and meowed, like it was asking me to pet it.

No way. No freaking way. It'll probably bite off my finger.

I loved cats... but not ones that appeared out of nowhere in a labyrinth the gods had created in a game designed to kill me. However, the cat made no sudden moves. I could always shoot a bolt of lightning at it and incinerate it before it had a chance to do anything bad. But I couldn't harm a potentially innocent animal. I doubted anything *innocent* awaited me in the labyrinth, but there was no way I was attacking the cat first.

Anyway, maybe it wasn't there to kill me.

"Is there something you want to show me?" I asked the cat, speaking softly again to avoid being heard by Octavia or Felix.

It stood up, meowed, and turned into the right side of the path. It walked forward, its tail moving as if motioning for me to follow.

The cat was sent to me by the gods.

The gods wanted me to go right.

So I glared at one of the orbs, turned left, and picked up my pace.

I needed to stop getting distracted by shiny swords and sweet cats.

Because the longer I spent slowly exploring the maze, the more time Octavia and Felix had to find each other so they could gang up against me.

42

SELENA

THERE WERE MORE SHINY, sky blue weapons designed for me. There was an adorable Pomeranian puppy. There was a stunning group of gold and silver butterflies that landed on my arms and tried to get me to follow them. There was a dead end with a garden of roses that smelled so sweet I was tempted to lie down in it and breathe in the heavenly aroma. There was even a platter of colorful bite sized cakes that made my stomach rumble just from looking at them.

I ignored it all and marched forward, continuing with the plan of always turning right—unless the creatures tried pulling me in another direction. Then I went against them.

I turned into another dead end, with another garden.

Felix was lying in the middle of this one. He'd pulled

a bunch of roses toward his nose, smiling as he inhaled their sweet scent. A rose quartz sword was on the ground in front of the garden.

Lightning crackled in my palms, and a breeze blew against my face. It would only take one long, forceful bolt from my hands to kill him.

I raised my hands and gathered my magic.

Then, he turned his head and looked straight at me.

I waited for him to get up and grab his sword. It would be less of a burden on my conscience if I killed him while he was pointing a weapon at me.

But he just smiled and continued lying there, defenseless.

"Selena," he drawled, his voice silky smooth. "Aren't you going to go find Octavia?"

I stepped forward. "You know I could easily kill you right now," I said.

"You could. But you won't."

I narrowed my eyes, not letting my guard down. Because Felix *was* fighting, in his unique way. With his words. He was trying to lure me into conversation. He was trying to distract me.

I spun around, ready for Octavia to jump out and attack. But there was no sign of her. And the hedge behind me closed, trapping Felix and me in the creepy fae garden.

"Get up," I said, and surprisingly, he did.

Once he was standing, he opened one of his hands. Crumpled rose petals fell out and fluttered to the ground. "Smells delicious, doesn't it?" he asked.

I stood there, saying nothing.

"I thought I'd lie there until you and Octavia finished duking it out," he continued. "I still can. You know they want to see a fight—a real fight. If you try to leave, the hedge will probably open back up for you."

He truly was a meek, pathetic little mouse. "You weren't even going to try to find her?" I asked.

He looked baffled. "Why would I do that?"

"To help her," I said. "You might not be much of a fighter, but I didn't expect you to just…" I glanced at the garden behind him and the sword still at his feet, since I wasn't sure *what* he was doing. Enjoying himself, from the look of it.

"She was already here." He smirked. "I let her have some fun with me in these flowers. Let out some stress, if you will. Then I sent her back off to find you. Given your arrival here now, I guess she wasn't successful."

The sight of the crushed roses in the garden made me even more disgusted than it had before. "You're a sad excuse for a man," I said. "Lounging around here instead of trying to help the person you claim to love."

"My presence would be more of a hindrance to her

than a help." He shrugged. "She'd be worried for me, which would take away her focus from trying to kill you."

"Trying to turn your cowardice into selflessness." My words were as sharp as steel. "Pathetic. Pick up your sword. At least *try* to fight me. Maybe the blade will be strong enough to deflect lightning." I smiled as electricity danced around my fingertips, taunting him.

He glanced at the sword, but made no move to pick it up. "It's a shame you're immune to my powers." He stepped over his sword and prowled toward me with a predatory gaze that he probably thought was seductive.

My magic lit up my hands and arms, stopping him before he got too close.

"You're beautiful, Selena," he continued, tilting his head and studying me. "We could have had fun together, you and I. We could still have fun together, here in these flowers. Let me give you some pleasure before your final fight. Just like I did for Octavia."

He reached forward to touch my cheek, and I flinched back.

Enough was enough.

I pushed my lightning out of my palms and hit Felix in the chest, throwing him backward. He convulsed, his eyes bloodshot and wide, his body a bright lightbulb of electricity. I moved my hands higher, and the lightning moved with them, lifting him off the ground and pushing him further back until he hovered above the rose garden. His eyes rolled back in his head as he seized, and I threw more magic into the bolt, sending it into his heart.

Finally, he stilled.

But hurricane-force rage swirled within me. Rage at Felix, at Octavia, at Prince Devyn, at the gods, at the Games, and even at my parents, for never telling me the truth of what I was. I held onto the bolt, releasing more and more magic into it, holding Felix's dead body up in the air as it shook and blackened.

"Stop!" someone called from behind me. "He's dead. Please, just stop."

I released the last of my lightning, and Felix's charred body dropped into the garden. The flowers touching him turned black and disintegrated. His hair was gone, and his skin was so burned that it was impossible to tell it was him.

I turned around slowly. The hedge had re-opened the path, and Octavia stood in the entrance.

Tears rolled down her cheeks, her chest heaving as she tried and failed to hold them back.

I held her gaze, waiting for her to attack. If she did, that would be it. Attacking another champion in the arena after one of the three was dead was against the rules. She'd immediately be eliminated.

But even when she was inches away from hysteria, Octavia was smarter than that. A few long, deep breaths, and she regained control.

"I hate you," she snarled, baring her teeth at me like she was a shifter. "And I'm glad I saw the end of what you did to him. How you attacked him even after he was dead. Because now, I'm more ready than ever to kill you."

43

SELENA

EVERYTHING AROUND ME BLURRED. The ground disappeared from under my feet, and I was floating in a void of nothingness. It was similar to how it felt when being teleported by a witch.

My vision cleared a few seconds later.

I was back inside the glass box. The door was closed, and I was staring out at the path lined with hedges.

I knew the gods were powerful. But did they just send me back in time?

My breaths came faster, the glass walls more confining than ever. I looked around in panic.

Felix's family was gone from their box. Julian was gone from the Royal Box.

I hadn't been sent back in time. Of course I hadn't.

Supernaturals were capable of a lot, but time travel was impossible.

Bacchus floated in his chariot in the center of the Coliseum. "Felix—the chosen champion of Venus—has been defeated!" he said, his voice booming through the arena. "His soul is on its way to Elysium, where he'll be honored as a god for all eternity. May his crossing to the Underworld be a peaceful one!"

"May his crossing to the Underworld be a peaceful one!" the crowd said in unison.

Bacchus was solemn for a few seconds. Then, he grinned. "But the fun is only just beginning," he said. "Who's ready for the final fight of this year's Faerie Games?"

The crowd erupted with excitement. Faerie fruit and colorful rose petals floated down from the canopied ceiling and into their waiting hands. Honey wine rained down, and the fae raised their glasses to catch it. It only stopped raining wine once their glasses were overflowing.

"As you know, this arena fight is different from the previous ones," Bacchus continued. "Because the chosen champions of Neptune, Mars, and Jupiter will fight until only one of them is alive. And that champion will be the winner of this year's Faerie Games!"

More applause. Glasses clinked together, and wine

was chugged. Feet stomped so intensely that the ground shook.

"But this maze will be different than the previous one." Bacchus pointed the pinecone tip of his scepter downward. Purple magic came out of it with the force of a smoke machine, until my glass box was surrounded by it. All I saw was purple.

The mist lifted, and the green, flowery hedges no longer lined the path. They'd been replaced with twisted, gnarled branches wound so tightly together that they were as solid as walls. The path was narrower, darker, and more sinister. An eerie shiver ran up and down my spine at the thought of stepping foot inside of it.

The gods and the fae don't want to see monsters kill the champions, Vejovis's words from earlier echoed through my mind. *They want to see the champions kill each other.*

I couldn't let the new surroundings affect me. The only true threat in that creepy maze was going to be Octavia.

"That's better." Bacchus looked mighty pleased with himself as he admired the maze. "Now, let the final fight begin!"

The glass door swung open. And just like last time, when I stepped onto the ground, the cheering crowd disappeared.

I didn't waste time trying to jump to see an overview of the maze. I needed to be faster this time. So I ran down the first path, turned right, and then turned right again. On my third right, I reached a dead end.

An ocean blue, crystal key emerged from the twisted branches and floated at waist height before me. The same color as Octavia's wings. It was slightly larger than my hands, and the top of it was decorated in curly spirals.

What does it mean?

I didn't know. But Felix had taken his sword in the previous maze, and it hadn't seemed to have done anything bad to him. Maybe I should take it? It was only a key. How could it harm me?

Plus, leaving without the key didn't feel right.

I glanced up at where Prince Devyn sat stoically in the Royal Box. His eyes were fixed on me, but he made no attempt of motioning to give me a clue.

Trust yourself and your instincts. Do that, and you'll have the best chance at winning the Games.

He'd said that to me when he'd told me he was nominating me for the Faerie Games. And right now, my instincts were telling me to take the key.

I ran down the path and grabbed it before I could overthink it. I held my breath, waiting for something terrible to happen. But nothing did.

Okay, I thought. *You're fine. Totally fine. It's just a key. It's not going to hurt you.*

I examined it, trying to find some sort of clue about what to use it for. But there was nothing.

Looked like I'd have to keep exploring the labyrinth.

Holding onto the key, I ran through the passages, continuing with my plan to always go right. No animals approached me, no butterflies landed on me, and I didn't come across any gardens or food. The dark maze was utterly and completely dead.

I had no sense of where I was. But just when I was thinking about retracing my steps, I turned into a dead end that led straight to a steel gray door embedded in the trees. The door was slightly taller than me, and rounded at the top. Twisted, dead vines grew on the gnarled branches around it. And a big keyhole was right above the handle.

I ran forward and shoved my key inside of it. But when I tried to turn it, it didn't budge.

Of course it didn't. The key was Octavia's color, and the door was Julian's color. I probably needed a matching key to open the door. And I didn't know where the doors would lead, but I'd feel much more comfortable testing it out by going through Julian's door than through Octavia's.

Why do I even need a key? I thought, my electricity

humming through my veins. *I can use my magic to blast the door open.*

I raised my other hand and shot an explosive bolt of lightning at the door.

The wood charred, but didn't break. So I shot another bolt, holding it and putting more magic into it. Again, it left only a dark, charred circle in its wake.

Frustration raged through me, and I shot another bolt at the thick wall of branches above the door. If I couldn't break through the door, maybe I could break through the wall.

Another charred circle.

I was wasting time.

I needed to find Julian's key.

I exited the dead end and continued keeping right as I ran through the maze. Unlike the previous maze, the walls weren't shifting in this one. My strategy of staying to the right should have been working. But it felt like it was taking *forever*.

Finally, I came across another dead end with a key. A *steel gray* key.

I ran forward and grabbed it. The moment I did, the ocean blue key disappeared from my hand and re-appeared where the gray one had been floating. I reached for the blue key, and the gray key took its spot again.

I could only hold onto one key at a time.

So I grabbed Julian's key again. Octavia's took its place, and I headed out of the dead end.

If I'd gotten to Julian's key by always turning right, then I should be able to find his door again by only turning left.

I kept to the left and ran faster, ready to open Julian's door and discover what was behind it. Hopefully, it would be him. Then we could team up and take down Octavia together.

Finally, I reached the dead end.

The door in front of me was ocean blue. And it had a charred circle above it.

I was in the same place as before. But *the doors had moved.*

I looked down at Julian's key in my hand, knowing it wouldn't open Octavia's door. I tried anyway, and sure enough, it didn't budge.

Crap. Crap, crap, crap.

Wind whipped around me as I stared at the door. If I hated mazes before, I *despised* them now.

But angrily standing there wasn't getting me any closer to unlocking Julian's door. So, key in hand, I ran forward. This time, I took whichever path I wanted. I ran and ran and ran, but everything blended together. I was sweating now, more lost and frustrated than ever.

The walls felt like they were closing in around me. The paths all looked the same, and none of them were leading me anywhere. Worse, I was close to positive that I'd been running through the same passages over and over. And given that I'd yet to run into either Octavia or Julian, I suspected I could only find them by opening one of those damn doors.

I shot another angry bolt at the wall, leaving a black circle behind.

And then, I felt like the biggest idiot in the world.

Because I could sporadically char the walls to mark where I'd been. Like Hansel and Gretel leaving bread-crumbs to mark their path.

Refreshed by the new idea, I continued running, shooting bolts at the walls. I finally felt like I was onto something.

Then I ended up back at the place where Octavia's key floated in the air.

I shot a bolt at the wall above the key. It would have been *so* satisfying to blow the key to smithereens, but I'd learned my lesson with the orbs on the first day of the Games.

That felt like ages ago. I hadn't come this far to be eliminated now.

So I picked myself back up and kept going.

Finally, after I was pretty sure I'd exhausted every possible path, I found it.

Julian's door.

I shoved the key into the lock, turned it, and opened the door. I was greeted with a wall of thick, hazy gray fog. I squinted and tried to see through it, but I couldn't make out a thing.

I glanced over my shoulder. No way was I going to keep running around in circles in that awful maze.

But what if this was a trick? What if, by going through Julian's door, I'd somehow end up pitting myself against him?

I had no idea. But Julian's door felt safer than Octavia's. It felt *right*. Plus, it had taken me forever to get there with the right key. If I turned around, who knew how long it would take me to find Octavia's key again and make it to her door?

Julian and Octavia could already be fighting each other while I was lost in the maze, asking myself questions I couldn't answer.

Wind whooshed past my ears. *Go*, I could almost hear it whisper.

So I gathered my magic in my hands, kept my eyes straight ahead, and stepped into the steel gray mist.

SELENA

Julian and Octavia were fighting in a ring lined with the brown, twisted walls from the maze. We were right in the center of the arena, and the crowd had reappeared around us. They were clapping and cheering, but I couldn't hear them.

There were so many footsteps on the wet, muddy ground that I assumed the two of them had been at it for a while.

They were fighting similarly to how they had in the Minotaur competition. But unlike then, they weren't holding back. Octavia was attacking with water and ice, while Julian held her off with a sword and a shield. She was fast, but he was faster. Her icicles shattered and melted against his impossibly strong weapons. Once used, the water evaporated, returning to the air she'd drawn it from.

They were close enough together that I couldn't shoot lightning at her without risking Julian getting caught in the crossfire. That was the hardest part of fighting two against one. Attacking your opponent without accidentally landing a blow on your teammate.

Julian continued fending off her attacks, but he couldn't get close enough for a killing blow. Sweat dampened Octavia's hairline. Julian looked like he could go at it all day. By letting her constantly be on the attack, he was wearing her down.

It wouldn't be long before she slowed enough for him to finish her off.

Finally, she saw me. She held one palm out to face me, the other out to Julian, and shot forceful streams of water at both of us.

Julian blocked it with his shield.

I held out my hands and shot my lightning down to the ground, creating a ring of electricity around me.

Her water sizzled and evaporated on contact.

She continued attacking both of us at once, but we deflected everything she threw at us. And now that she was splitting her efforts, Julian was moving in on her.

Wind whipped around me, and thunder rumbled in

the sky. With each burst of water and ice that Octavia threw at me, the electric ring around me grew.

But Julian was only a sword's length away from driving his blade through her heart. So she had no choice but to turn all her efforts to defending herself against him.

She protected her chest against his sword with a shield of ice, snarling as he used his shield to deflect the water shooting out of her other hand. Hate raged in her eyes. The same hate as when she'd tortured and killed Cassia.

My body thrummed with magic, the pressure of it intensifying and pushing out against my skin. It didn't want to be contained. No—*I* didn't want to keep it contained.

I screamed and raised my hands in the air. My ring of electricity grew into a dome. And there was still so much magic inside of me. It sizzled and popped, begging to be released.

Octavia was right to fear me from the beginning.

But if I let my magic loose now, it wouldn't only be Octavia who suffered.

"Julian!" I called, creating an opening in my electric dome.

Octavia's ice shield was cracking. Julian was moments away from killing her. But he must have seen something in my eyes, because he threw his shield against her magic with so much strength that it forced past her water stream, crashed into her, and slammed her against the wall.

Sword in hand, he ran and joined me inside the dome before she had a chance to get up.

I sealed the door the moment he was in.

"Selena," he said, and he reached forward, stopping inches away from my glowing skin. "What are you—"

I didn't hear the rest of his question.

Because I raised my palms to the sky, and electricity exploded out of me like an atomic bomb. The ground was soaked with the remnants of Octavia's water, and my lightning *fed* on it, eating up everything in its path.

The bright white light was blinding. Thunder boomed so loudly that the ground shook. A tornado of wind whipped my hair across my cheeks. The sharp smell of smoke consuming wood filled the air.

The light flashed out, and everything stilled.

Exhaustion weighed down my body. Depleted of energy, I fell to my knees and dropped my hands to the ground. Julian kneeled down next to me and wrapped his arms around me, holding me up as I surveyed my surroundings.

All that remained of Octavia was a pile of ash. The ring where we'd been fighting was charred black, and the labyrinth was gone. Disintegrated into mounds of ash. The only untouched place on the arena floor was the small circle around Julian and me.

Flakes of ash floated down onto my cheeks and hair. I looked up, and saw that the canopy ceiling of the Coliseum was gone as well. Burned.

The crowd was stunned into silence. Many of the fae held their hands in the air, their magic joined together to create a rainbow barrier that extended over everyone in the audience. Even over the half-bloods.

I'd focused my magic on the arena floor and up at the sky, purposefully keeping it away from the crowd. I was relieved that it had worked, or at least that the fae were able to protect themselves. Because most of the fae out there weren't responsible for the existence of the Games. And if my instinct was right, their bloodlust was influenced by Bacchus's magic. Plus, there were children out there, and half-bloods, too. Julian's family—who were now *my* family—was out there.

I wouldn't have been able to live with myself if anyone in the crowd had died because of me. And while I'd been forced to kill in the Faerie Games to keep myself and Julian alive, Bridget, Felix, and Octavia's deaths would weigh on my conscience forever.

The fae must have realized I wasn't a danger now that I was a crumpled mess on the ground, because they slowly lowered their shields until the rainbow barrier was gone.

With the barrier gone, ash floated down upon them, too. They looked up at it in wonder. They clearly hadn't expected that much magic from a half-blood—even from one that was a chosen champion.

Still trying to catch my breath, I buried myself deeper in Julian's arms. But I didn't turn my face away from the crowd. All I could hear was Julian's steady breathing, and his heart racing in his chest. Except for the ash floating down from the sky, everything was still.

Then, Bacchus circled his chariot overhead. "Octavia —the chosen champion of Neptune—has been defeated!" His cheery voice filled the arena, out of place in the eerie silence. "Her soul is on its way to Elysium, where she'll be honored as a goddess for all eternity. May her crossing to the Underworld be a peaceful one!"

The fae slowly turned their attention back to the god. "May her crossing to the Underworld be a peaceful one," a few of them said, followed by the rest of them. But they were far less excited than before.

Bacchus looked around, troubled. "More wine!" he said with a forced laugh. He raised his scepter, and honey wine rained down.

The fae who caught it looked into their glasses in disgust. None of them drank.

I assumed the wine had been polluted with ash.

Bacchus frowned and lowered his scepter. "But we're not done yet!" he said. "Who's ready to see our final two fight, and this year's winning champion rise?!"

The first few rows of fae cheered. And then, like it was contagious, the rest of the audience cheered, too. The only ones not cheering were Julian's family and Empress Sorcha.

Julian held me tighter. "Can you stand?" he murmured in my ear.

"Yes," I said, even though I wasn't sure. My muscles ached, like after pushing myself too hard in a training session.

But I fought the pain and forced myself up, grateful for Julian's help. I kept my eyes locked on his the entire time. The ash streaked his face like war paint, and I hoped I looked as fierce as he did.

Once we were standing, he kept an arm firmly around my waist and looked straight up at Bacchus. "We love each other," he said to the god. "And no matter what you might say to us, or what you might do to us, we won't raise a hand against each other."

Some people in the crowd laughed. Some clapped. Others were silent.

"So it's going to be one of *those* finales." Bacchus sighed and glanced to the sky. "JUNO! Your turn."

The clouds parted, and Juno floated down on her peacock-feathered throne. The top of her scepter glowed blue, and the ash stopped falling as she descended. Her bright, pure gold gown glimmered in the sunlight.

Bacchus moved his chariot over to get out of her way.

The throne settled down next to the pile of ash that had been Octavia. It was as tall as a house, since Juno hadn't bothered to shrink herself down to our height.

Now that I was facing her, determination coursed through me. I felt steadier on my feet. After all, I'd just decimated the entire labyrinth. I refused to look weak in front of her.

Julian must have felt the change in me, because he unwound his arm from around my back and held my hand instead.

"Selena," Juno said, her face giving away no emotion. "Julian. I see the two of you are refusing to participate in the final fight of the Faerie Games."

She was so calm that it was scary.

"We are," Julian said.

"Well, that just won't do." She crossed her legs and sat back in her throne. "The final two are required by the rules of the Games to fight to the death. Break that rule, and I'll have no choice but to kill you both."

"You have a choice," I said, and she sat back in shock. I continued before I could second-guess myself for talking back to a goddess. "You made the rules of the Games. Is there a rule that you can't change them?"

"I technically can," she said. "But why should I? It's far more entertaining to force your hand." She looked around at the crowd and smiled. "Don't you all agree?"

Only about half of them clapped.

"You can do better than that. Don't you all agree?!" she repeated, louder.

There were a few more claps. But not many.

Juno's smiled vanished, and she looked back at me and Julian like she was about to smite us on the spot.

"They don't want us to fight because it doesn't feel right to them," Julian said, his voice gaining intensity as he spoke. "They might not understand why yet, but I'd bet most of them can tell that our feelings for each other run deeper than mortal love. Because it's a love that many of them have experienced themselves. The unbreakable, eternal bond of soulmates."

45

SELENA

THE CROWD GASPED.

Juno looked unmoved. Of course she did. She knew all of this already.

But the fae in the audience didn't. This was more for them than for her. Because if they wanted Julian and I to stay alive, maybe Juno would listen.

"Prove it," she finally said.

"Fine." Julian lowered his breeches an inch to reveal the clover birthmark on his left hipbone. An orb buzzed forward to get a close-up, broadcasting it so everyone could see.

It wasn't so easy in my dress. I'd planned to use my electricity to burn a slit through the material, but when I dug inside of myself, there were still only embers. It was like the first time I'd tried using my magic. It was there, but I couldn't quite grasp it.

Julian pulled a small blade out of the ether to help me. But I didn't take it. Because even though I knew the fae couldn't doubt the strength of my magic after the show I'd just given them, I wanted to do this myself. I was *going* to do this myself.

Then, I felt it. A spark. A small one, but it was enough for me to harness.

"You're the goddess of family," I said to Juno, my hand slowly lighting up with electricity. "And being soulmates means being family."

I ran my index finger over my left hipbone, burning a modest slit through the jeweled material. I opened it and revealed my birthmark that matched Julian's.

The orb zoomed in on it, and the audience went wild.

"You can't force them to kill each other!"

"They really *are* soulmates."

"I knew there was something different about them!"

"Make a new rule!"

That last phrase caught on, and it wasn't long before the crowd was chanting it in unison. The fae with soulmates—which was about three-fourths of them—held their clasped hands up in the air as they repeated the words over and over again.

I reached for Julian's hand and held it tight. The support of the crowd gave me hope, and I stared up at Juno, praying for mercy.

She slammed her staff onto the ground. "SILENCE!" she said, and the entire arena hushed. She glared over her shoulder at Bacchus. Then she returned her focus to me and Julian, her eyes hard. "This is an... unexpected surprise," she finally said. "However, I'm not the one who marks soulmates. That honor goes to Venus. So it's only fair to consult with her before making a decision."

I expected Juno to float back up into the sky and leave Julian and me waiting as she spoke with Venus.

Instead, Venus descended down in an iridescent pearl clamshell. Her long blond hair was perfectly curled, and she wore a sheer nude dress with beads covering her more personal areas.

"Venus," Juno scolded her. "What is the meaning of this?"

"The meaning of what?" She smiled demurely, since they both knew exactly what the other was talking about. This performance was for the crowd.

"Of marking two players in the Faerie Games as soulmates."

"I don't simply decide who's going to be soulmates on a whim," she said, pulling her hair to the front and pushing out her breasts. "I innately sense it. The soulmate bond is holy, and it's one of my jobs to make sure soulmates can find each other."

"You heard her!" shouted a fae in the crowd.

"The bond is holy!"

"They can't kill each other!"

Juno eyed them angrily. "Hush," she said, and they did. "I called Venus down to listen to her. Interruptions are nothing but a hindrance."

They shuffled around as they took their seats.

Juno turned back to Venus. "As you see, the citizens of the Otherworld are less than thrilled about pitting soulmates against each other," she said, her tone laced with annoyance. "And the Games *are* designed for entertainment. The soulmate bond between these two puts us in quite the predicament."

"That it does," Venus agreed. "But like I said, the soulmate bond is holy. Pitting soulmates against each other is unnatural, to say the least."

"I could smite them and send them straight to Elysium." Juno shrugged. "That would solve the problem."

"Please, don't," I begged. "There's no rule in the Games regarding soulmates."

"You can make a new rule that allows both of us to live," Julian said, motioning to the crowd. "After all, it seems to be what they want."

The crowd clapped in approval.

Juno gave them a spiteful look, and they silenced once more.

"They make a good point," Venus said, and then, she *winked* at us. "There's no rule in the Games that says you can't create a new rule. And this is the first time in the history of the Faerie Games that soulmates have been chosen to compete. It makes sense that a new circumstance deserves a new rule."

"Perhaps," Juno said, and I could practically see the wheels spinning in her mind as she continued to study Julian and me.

"Would you ever be able to kill your husband?" Julian asked. "Jupiter?"

Juno scowled, and Julian's grip around my hand tightened. He was pushing this. But even though we'd sworn to fight the gods before fighting each other, I knew it would be futile. We might be powerful, but we had nothing on the gods. And I was so depleted of magic that it would be silly to even try.

We needed to convince her with our words.

"Mars's chosen champion asks a fair question," Venus said. Given her light tone, it was clear she was enjoying this. "Every time Jupiter has been unfaithful, you've taken it out on the women who caught his eye. Never on him. Why is that?"

Juno pressed her lips into a firm line. She held her

intimidating gaze with mine, and I did my best to stand steady and strong.

"Jupiter's appreciation for alluring young women is certainly an annoyance," she finally said. "Of course, when he finally chose a champion, it was a beautiful maiden. I hated you for that."

Frustrated tears welled in my eyes, and I swallowed them down. "I don't know why Jupiter chose me," I said. "But Julian's my soulmate. I love him. I'd never betray him."

"I believe you." Juno rested an elbow on her throne and smirked. "And knowing this makes me hate you less. I might even go as far as saying it makes me like you."

I froze, stunned.

I didn't know what I was expecting her to say. But it certainly hadn't been *that*.

"Why's that?" I was treading on thin ice, and I needed to do it carefully.

"Since you have a soulmate, my husband can never win your love, even if he tried," she said simply. "This amuses me greatly."

Hope rose in my chest, and I felt Julian's pulse quicken.

Did our plea actually work?

"Therefore, I've come to a decision." Juno sat

straighter and held her staff firmly by her side. "I'm going to grant your request, and create a new rule for the Games."

46

SELENA

THE CROWD STOOD and erupted into cheers.

My heart leaped. I turned to Julian and wanted to kiss him right there, despite the fae and the gods watching us.

But he still looked worried.

Why?

Juno raised a hand, and the crowd sat down again. "Not so fast," she said, and I turned back to her, trying to push down the pit of worry growing in my stomach. "I still need to announce what this new rule is."

I stepped closer to Julian, and he wrapped an arm around my shoulders.

Please be a rule in our favor, I prayed.

I couldn't bring myself to look at Julian's family, but I was sure they were praying, too.

"If soulmated champions are the only two left standing in the Games, they won't be required to fight to the death," Juno said, eliciting more cheers from the audience.

Every cell in my body froze, in both excitement that Julian and I wouldn't have to fight, and in anticipation of what Juno was going to say next. The crowd must have felt the same way, because instead of standing again, they sat anxiously on the edges of their seats.

Bacchus drove his chariot down to the center of the arena and settled himself next to Juno. "The Games can only have one winner," he said, leaning lazily back in his plush seat. "It's one of the rules. It would be boring to have *two*."

Juno narrowed her eyes at him in a lethal death stare. "As Jupiter and Mars's champions pointed out, there's no rule saying I can't change the rules," she said. "And besides, I didn't ask for your opinion."

Bacchus opened his mouth to speak, but then closed it.

Apparently satisfied, Juno turned away from him. "As I was saying, the soulmated champions won't be killed, at least not immediately," she continued, and my heart stopped. *Not immediately* didn't sound positive. "They'll be sent on a challenging, dangerous quest to prove they both deserve to win the Faerie Games.

Succeed on the quest, and they'll live. Fail, and they'll die."

My heart pounded as a myriad of emotions ran through me at once. Relief that Julian and I wouldn't have to fight today. Gratefulness to be shown mercy. But also, worry that we'd be sent on an impossible quest.

I wouldn't put it past the gods and the fae to toy with us like that.

But Julian and I were strong on our own, and even stronger together. We'd complete whatever they threw at us.

We *had* to. There was no escape. The gods would hunt us down and smite us if we tried to run.

Julian stood strong beside me, and I knew he was thinking the same thing.

Bacchus sat up in his chariot, his eyes lighting up again. "I suppose there are worse things than hosting a quest," he said, sipping from a glass of wine that he'd pulled from the ether. "They're always entertaining."

"There will be no need for a host." Juno smiled knowingly. "I want the champions to have their best chance at completing the quest without outside distractions. Which means no orbs, and no broadcast. You'll be sent on your way to do… well, whatever it is you do."

He scowled at her, but didn't argue.

"I want the quest to benefit the Otherworld," she

continued, and people in the audience murmured in approval. "Therefore, I won't be selecting their task. That honor will go to your Empress, Sorcha."

All eyes went to the Royal Box, where Sorcha sat proudly on her throne. The orbs buzzed around her, and her expression was serene, as always. As if she'd expected this.

Prince Devyn also appeared calm.

Had he known this would happen? Had he warned her?

"Empress," Juno said to her. "Do you require time to decide their task, or do you already know what you want them to do?"

Sorcha tilted her head, her pale eyes glimmering in the conniving way of the fae. "I can take as much time as I'd like?" she asked in her childlike voice.

"Of course not," Juno said. "One month will be sufficient. Shall we reconvene when you're ready?"

"No need. I already know what I want them to do." She stood, and everyone in the audience stood, too. Juno and Bacchus were the only ones who remained seated. "Upon exiting the Coliseum, Julian and Selena will be exiled from the citadel," she said, looking straight at us. "They can only return by bringing back the First Queen's Holy Wand."

The crowd took a collective breath inward.

And then, uproar.

"A death sentence!" someone screamed from the back.

"The plague is out there!"

"They won't survive it!"

"They'll be eaten alive!"

"The Holy Wand is a myth! It doesn't exist!"

As they argued, I turned to Julian, my eyes wide.

"What's wrong?" he asked.

"There's a prophecy on Avalon," I said, unsure where to begin. "It's too much to explain now. But it involves a Holy Wand."

His forehead creased, and I could tell I'd caught him by surprise. "Interesting," he finally said. "We'll have time—and privacy—once we're outside of the city's walls. Tell me then."

I nodded, too awestruck to say any more. Because the people in the audience saying that the wand didn't exist were wrong. Our prophetess's vision from all those years ago would be too much of a coincidence otherwise.

Sorcha stared at the audience as they bickered amongst themselves, letting them continue until they quieted on their own.

Once they were silent, she turned her focus to Julian

and me. "My decision is final," she said, giving us a small, encouraging smile. "I wish the two of you the best of luck."

47

SORCHA

As ALWAYS, I'd gathered my closest friends and advisors to celebrate the end of the Games at my country villa.

I lounged on the largest settee in the yard, sipping my drink as I watched the musicians play and the nobility dance in the moonlight. Everyone wore their finest silks and gems, and most had gotten drunk hours ago. Those not dancing relaxed at the banquet tables, enjoying overflowing spreads of fruit, cheese, jams, and sweetmeats. Everyone's wings sparkled brightly after watching such an exciting finale of the Faerie Games.

At some point in the night, most of the guests had approached me to toast in Selena and Julian's favor. I'd happily raised my glass and returned their well wishes.

Little did they know that I was drinking lychee juice instead of wine.

A few of the younger fae who'd yet to find their soulmates cozied up around me, flirting and competing for my favor. I appeased them, smiling at all the expected times and giving them an equal amount of attention. I'd even granted a fae boy's request for a taste of my magical gift. *Bliss*, they called it.

He was now lying in the grass, his eyes half-closed as he gazed at the stars.

I was braiding a young fae's golden hair when a shadow stopped over us. I paused my braiding and looked up into the familiar gray eyes of Aeliana. She was the first chosen champion of Minerva's to ever win the Faerie Games, and one of my most trusted advisors.

She bowed her head. "Your Highness," she said.

"Aeliana," I replied, and only then did she meet my eyes again.

"May I have a word?" she asked. "In private?"

I sighed, as if I couldn't bear to be pulled away from the revelry. "If you must." I returned my attention to the fae surrounding me and shooed them off. "Go, have fun," I said. "I'll find you when it pleases me."

I stood up to walk with Aeliana, and everyone who was seated in the yard stood as well—even the drunkest of them. I heard them shuffling to sit back down once I'd entered the villa and closed the door behind me.

I brought Aeliana to my bedroom, since it was the

most private space in the villa. Once inside, I sat in my armchair next to the blazing hearth. She sat in the chair across from me. There was a platter of colorful fruit on the table, but I made no move to take anything. Therefore, she didn't, either.

"I had a vision," she said once we were both settled.

"I assumed so," I said.

"I was going to wait until tomorrow to tell you, but it seemed as though..."

"As though I needed a break?" I smiled to let her know it was all right.

"Yes." She cleared her throat, back to business. "I saw the afflicted fae crossing the western mountains and leaving the Wild Lands."

I clasped my hands in my lap and maintained a cool exterior, despite the concern weighing on my chest. "I feared as much when we lost contact with the town of Trajan," I said.

"If they continue on this path, they'll cross the central plains and continue toward the citadel." Aeliana lowered her eyes, clearly not enjoying being the messenger of such unwelcome information.

"At least they're still on the other side of the continent," I said brightly. "Do you know how long it would take them to make their way here?"

"At the rate the plague is spreading, we likely have a

few weeks," she said. "But since we've never seen anything like this, it's impossible to say for sure."

"This complicates matters."

"It does," she agreed. "I advise that you gather the strongest royal fae to fortify the magical boundary around the citadel. I can't ensure that it will keep out the afflicted, but I doubt it will hurt."

"Defensive measures this early on will cause unnecessary panic and chaos," I said. "We still have contact with the town of Hadrian. If they go dark, I'll strengthen the boundary. Until then, we'll keep everyone calm until we find a cure, or at least until we learn how to immobilize the afflicted fae."

She took a deep breath and forced a smile. "The show must go on," she said.

"Yes." I paused to listen to the quickening violin music outside. "Did you see anything in your vision regarding those we sent to investigate the plague?"

"Unfortunately not," she said. "They're still missing. Our best hope remains in Selena and Julian finding that wand."

"Then let's pray they succeed." I gazed into the flames, thinking back to a pivotal conversation I'd had with Prince Devyn over a millennia ago. "The fate of our realm may depend on it."

Will Selena and Julian complete their quest to find the Holy Wand? What *is* this mysterious plague, and what will happen if they stumble upon it?

Grab the next book in the series, The Faerie Wand, to find out! ➜ CLICK HERE or visit mybook.to/faeriewand

Check out the gorgeous cover below! (You may need to turn the page to see the cover.)

I thought I could return home once the Faerie Games were over. I was wrong.

Now, Julian and I must complete the dangerous quest given to us by the Empress of the Otherworld. The Holy Wand is out there. We just need to find it.

No matter where the journey takes us, we'll destroy anything blocking our path. We have to. Otherwise, we'll be dead.

Get your copy now at:
mybook.to/faeriewand

ABOUT THE AUTHOR

Michelle Madow is a USA Today bestselling author of fast paced fantasy novels that will leave you turning the pages wanting more! Her books are full of magic, adventure, romance, and twists you'll never see coming.

Click here or visit author.to/MichelleMadow to view a full list of Michelle's novels on Amazon.

To get free books, exclusive content, and instant updates

from Michelle, visit www.michellemadow.com/
subscribe and subscribe to her newsletter now!

THE FAERIE MATES

Published by Dreamscape Publishing

Copyright © 2019 Michelle Madow

ISBN: 9781670800626

This book is a work of fiction. Though some actual towns, cities, and locations may be mentioned, they are used in a fictitious manner and the events and occurrences were invented in the mind and imagination of the author. Any similarities of characters or names used within to any person past, present, or future is coincidental.

All rights reserved. No part of this book may be used or reproduced in any manner whatsoever without written permission from the author. Brief quotations may be embodied in critical articles or reviews.

❋ Created with Vellum

Made in the USA
Middletown, DE
13 February 2021

33676685R00198